HARD SHOT

J. B.
TURNER
HARD SHOT

THOMAS & MERCER

Published by Thomas & Mercer, Seattle

www.apub.com

Amazon, the Amazon logo, and Thomas & Mercer are trademarks of Amazon.com, Inc., or its affiliates.

ISBN-13: 9781542006132
ISBN-10: 1542006139

Cover design by @blacksheep-uk.com

Printed in the United States of America

For my late father

One

July 4

It was still dark when the white van pulled up opposite the Bronx courthouse.

Travis O'Keefe, sitting in the passenger seat, observed the dark, deserted street. He lit up his third cigarette of the day. His brother wound down the window.

"You wanna kill me with all that smoke," Ryan said, chomping on his nicotine gum.

"Quit whining, bro. Keep your eyes open."

Travis scanned the street. He had scouted this location for days. It was a perfect spot, directly opposite the entrance to the ten-story courthouse on Walton Avenue. The building's steel shutters were still down, the area deathly quiet.

A police siren broke the peace of the sultry early-morning air.

Ryan cranked up the air-conditioning. Travis watched a panhandler shuffle down the street, past the courthouse, and into the deli. A few moments later, the shutters of the courthouse rolled up. "Here we go."

They watched as the middle-aged black security guard they'd been surveilling for the last week headed off down the street, carrying his plain metal lunch box.

"About fucking time," Travis said.

Ryan was chewing hard on his gum.

"Wait till he's out of sight. Don't want him doubling back if he's forgotten something."

Ryan nodded. They waited for five more long minutes. "Let's do it."

The brothers got out. They wore blue maintenance coveralls and carried work bags. Travis pressed the security buzzer. He glanced up at the surveillance camera and smiled.

A voice on the intercom said, "We're closed. It's the Fourth of July."

"Sorry to bother you," Travis said. "We've got an emergency maintenance call."

The voice said, "No mention of that in the log."

"We've just been given the job, buddy. Air-conditioning on the roof."

"Who sent you?"

"The mayor's office. They're concerned there could be an electrical fault. We need to get up there and check it out. Could be a fire risk to the whole building."

The voice sighed. "Gimme a minute. I'll be down."

A few moments later, the doors opened.

A gray-haired white security guard was standing there yawning. "Couldn't this have waited?"

Ryan shook his head. "Sorry, but it's a priority."

"You got a work order or company ID?"

"Sure."

Travis pressed a gun to the man's head. "Inside!"

The man stumbled back as Travis pushed him into the building.

Ryan locked the front door, then hauled the terrified security guard down some stairs to a basement room. "Who else is on duty?"

"Just me."

"When does your replacement arrive?"

"Two p.m. National holiday, it's always just me."

2

Travis grinned, pointed the silenced handgun at the man, and shot him in the neck. The security guard was dead before he slammed face-first onto the ground. The sound of his nose cartilage being crushed was audible. Blood spilled onto the stone floor.

Ryan took the old man's keys from his pocket, locked the basement room so he wouldn't be found anytime soon, and turned to face his brother, eyes glazed. "You OK?"

Travis grinned. "I'm fine."

"What next?"

"Fresh air."

The two men took the elevator to the roof garden. Not a cloud in the sky. Not a breath of wind.

Travis looked around the huge roof. A ten-foot-high parapet wall surrounded it, conveniently shielding them from prying eyes.

The men got to work straightaway. They opened up their work bags. Inside were protective glasses and dust masks. They put them on and pulled out their power drills. Methodically, they began to drill two separate three-inch-wide holes through the wall, a couple yards apart.

Ryan peered through each of the holes. "Perfect line of sight. Check it out."

Travis followed suit, looking straight at Yankee Stadium. "It's going to be a beautiful day in New York City."

Two

The uptown 4 train jolted into motion.

Jon Reznick was sitting beside his daughter, Lauren, as the subway car screeched and rattled, gathering speed. Lauren wore a navy Yankees baseball cap and was flicking through messages on her phone. She looked flushed despite the air-conditioned carriage. "You OK, honey?"

"Dad, I'm fine. I just had too much to drink last night."

"What do I always tell you? Hydrate." Reznick handed her the bottle of water he was holding. "Drink it. You'll feel better."

Lauren took a few large gulps and returned the half-empty plastic bottle to him. "You worry too much."

"That's what parents are supposed to do. Worry. Especially dads with their daughters."

Lauren rolled her eyes. "Dad. I'm a grown adult."

"So, where were you drinking?"

"A place in the East Village."

"I know the East Village. That's where your mother and I had our first drink together. McSorley's."

Lauren smiled. "Yeah? I didn't know that."

"Where did you go?"

"It's a new place. Rooftop bar."

"Rooftop bar? Ugh, sounds awful."

She snorted. "What is it with you?"

"What do you mean?"

"You've got a real problem with fancy bars. Fancy places."

"Whatever floats your boat, I guess."

"It's a really nice place. Pretty hip new hotel. Great views from the terrace."

Reznick glanced at his watch. Then his gaze was drawn to the other passengers in the car. A wiry old white guy wearing full Yankees regalia, a few college kids, a family of German tourists, and twenty or so boisterous Yankee fans farther down the car. He faced his daughter. "Looking forward to the game?"

"Yeah, definitely."

"Section 216. Shaded. I checked."

She chuckled. "You're an obsessive."

"I'm particular. It's going to be blazing hot today. I don't want you sitting out in 100-degree heat without any shade."

She nudged his shoulder. "I changed my mind. You're not obsessive, you're a nightmare."

"You have no idea."

The train rumbled on through the Upper East Side and into Harlem.

Reznick was looking forward to spending his first full day in the city with his daughter. He'd flown down from Maine the day before and was staying at the Pierre, overlooking Central Park. He'd booked two rooms for him and Lauren. He'd thought it would make a nice change, as his daughter was currently sharing a cramped apartment with a couple of friends from the publishing company where she was interning for the second year on her summer break from Bennington. The previous night, they'd enjoyed a beautiful meal and a couple of drinks at the bar.

Reznick had been ready to call it a night, knowing they had the baseball game the following day. But Lauren had gotten a text from her friends—they were headed downtown to a club, and did she want to come? Reznick had hoped she would stay and shoot the breeze with him at the hotel, but no matter. He was just glad to get some precious time with her.

Reznick said, "So, when did you get back last night? I was worried about you."

"About four, I think. Maybe later."

"Are you kidding me? You must be exhausted."

"Don't say you've never partied, Dad."

She had him there. He remembered what it was like when he was in the Marines and would stay out late drinking. Getting up early the following morning was no fun. He took a sympathetic tack and simply said, "Glad you got home safely and had a good night."

Eventually, the train screeched, metal on metal, coming into the 161st Street station aboveground in the Bronx.

Reznick felt the blast of dirty steam-bath air as they stepped off the train and walked through the crowds. "Now remember," he said, "stay close. It's a sellout today. Fourth of July."

Lauren shook her head. "You need to relax, Dad. I'm an adult."

But she stuck close to him anyway. He resisted the urge to reach out and squeeze her hand. It was just last summer that he'd sat by her in the hospital while she lay in a coma. He understood her need to prove to herself that she no longer felt vulnerable. He hoped she understood that it would be a while before he no longer felt that way.

They headed down the subway stairs and out onto the broiling street. Cops stood everywhere, monitoring the crowds.

Reznick and Lauren edged through to join a huge line on the south side of Yankee Stadium. It snaked back at least a couple hundred yards from gates 4 and 6. An elevated train rumbled overhead, skirting the edge of the impressive new stadium. Lines of fans were also visible outside a McDonald's restaurant, virtually underneath the train track.

Reznick pulled his cap down to shield his eyes from the ferocious sun. He felt the sweat sticking to his T-shirt. It had to be at least 100 degrees already. "It's like a goddamn inferno today."

Lauren drank the rest of the bottle of water.

"Feel better?" he asked.

She smiled and hugged him tight. "I'm sorry I'm a little cranky today, Dad."

"Forget it. I just worry about you out on the streets of New York in the middle of the night."

"I caught an Uber with Shona. Besides, haven't you ever stayed out half the night?"

"Damn right I have. But I can look after myself. And I don't whine if I'm hungover."

"You really are stuck in the past, you do know that, right?"

Reznick smiled. "Is that such a bad thing? Traditional values?"

Lauren rolled her eyes. "Oh, come on. What does that even mean?"

A black guy selling large bottles of cold water sauntered past, wet towel draped over his head to protect himself from the blazing sun. "Get 'em while you can," he said. "Gotta keep cool, folks. The heat is gonna break records, they say."

Reznick bought two large bottles and gave the guy a ten-dollar bill.

"Thanks, man," the water seller said.

Reznick handed one of the bottles to his daughter. She took a few big gulps and poured the rest over her head to cool her down.

"Goddamn!" she said.

"Feeling better?" Reznick asked.

Lauren nodded, cheeks flushed. She put her Yankees hat back on.

Reznick turned and looked up at the stadium towering over them. "New York Yankees, Lauren," he said. "They were your mom's team. She used to go to the games as a little girl."

"I didn't know that."

Reznick shielded his eyes from the sun as the line began to inch forward. "Yeah, big baseball fan."

"We're going to have a great day today, Dad."

"You better believe it."

Three

Travis wiped the sweat from his forehead as the sun beat down onto the roof of the courthouse. He turned to his brother. "You ready?"

Ryan was chewing his nicotine gum. "Let's do it."

Travis screwed the two-and-a-half-inch suppressor onto the barrel of the rifle and adjusted his position, lying flat on the roof. He pulled his baseball cap low to shield his eyes from the sun. Slowly, he eased the sniper rifle through the carefully drilled hole in the parapet wall.

He looked through the scope. The crosshairs showed thousands of Yankee fans gathered outside the stadium, diagonally across from the courthouse, two hundred yards or so away.

He focused on the NYPD vehicles that had cordoned off the roads around the stadium, a routine on game days.

Travis looked at his watch. It was 10:55 a.m. Just over two hours before the Yankees would be taking on the Braves on Independence Day. Hundreds of baseball fans were already forming lines on the main concourse. The lines seemed to be getting longer by the minute as more and more people disembarked from the 161st Street station.

Travis's cell phone rang. He didn't recognize the caller ID.

"Hey, bro." The voice belonged to the shot caller. "You in place?"

"We're on the roof, awaiting the green light."

"How you feeling?"

"Feeling crazy. I want to get started."

"You want to taste blood, right?" the voice said.

"You know I do."

"Blood in, blood out, bro."

Travis knew what that meant. He had taken the oath. He had to follow orders. If not, he would be as good as dead. Those were the rules, and Travis had witnessed firsthand what happened when a member of their group broke their sacred code. Their blood oath. One poor fucker in Leavenworth had a tattoo on his arm that he hadn't earned the right to have.

They hadn't been able to get to him inside, so once Travis and Ryan were released, they lured the poor fuck from a bar, took him to a tow truck depot in New Jersey, and used a blowtorch to burn it off. The smell of the burning flesh never left Travis. Or the screaming of the guy who had betrayed them.

Travis cleared his throat. "So, I'm taking it this is a go?"

"That's right, bro. This is your fucking green light. Do it good. Don't let us down."

Travis ended the call and put the cell phone back in his pocket. He turned to Ryan. "It's a go."

Ryan lay down flat on the roof as he zeroed in on the first target.

Then Travis adjusted his position one final time. He looked through the crosshairs of the rifle. The first cop he spotted was drinking a bottle of water, leaning against his cruiser. Travis slid his finger onto the trigger. Then he opened fire.

Four

The sound of gunfire triggered instant panic outside the stadium.

Reznick grabbed Lauren by the arm and pulled her behind a pillar as people screamed, pushed, shoved, and fled in all directions, trying to take cover. He wrapped an arm around his daughter as chaos ensued. People were tripping over one another, trampling the poor souls who fell, and diving to the ground to escape the shots.

"Dad, what's happening!"

Reznick recognized the distinctive crack of high-velocity rounds. He saw people pointing to a building across the concourse. High up on the walled roof, Reznick could just make out a couple of glints in the sun. Was that the shooters, concealed from sight?

"Who's shooting, Dad? What the hell is going on?"

"I don't know. Could be a terrorist attack."

Lauren looked impassive. "Shit."

Reznick gripped her arms tight. "You OK?"

Lauren nodded. "Don't worry about me."

"Good girl. Time to move." Reznick hauled her to her feet, wrapped a protective arm around her as they ran for dear life in the direction everyone else was headed. He grabbed her wrist as they bounded down some stairs and stepped out into oncoming traffic. A yellow taxi screeched to a halt, inches from them.

The driver screamed out his window, "What the fuck, man? I'm trying to get out of here!"

"So is my daughter. Get her to safety!"

"What the hell is going on?"

"Active shooter situation."

"Get her in!" the driver shouted.

Reznick was crouched down on the driver's side and opened the rear door of the cab. He shoved Lauren, facedown, onto the floor. "Head down! Keep low!" More shots in the distance. "Head down! Keep low!"

Lauren turned around and fixed her gaze on him. "Don't get involved, Dad."

"Don't worry about me. Get back to the hotel. And stay there!"

A young Hispanic couple with two sons wearing Yankees shirts were crawling on the road near the cab. The boys were crying.

Reznick signaled them toward him. He grabbed the kids first and lifted them into the back of the cab, before ushering the grateful parents inside.

The mother was weeping. *"Gracias, señor."*

Reznick indicated for the woman to get her head down. "Out of sight!" He slammed the door shut.

He banged on the side of the cab and crouched down below the driver's open window. "Get the hell out of here! Move it!"

The cab sped away, narrowly avoiding mowing down a crowd of frightened people running across the street.

Reznick was relieved Lauren was hopefully out of harm's way along with the young family. He turned and stared up at the building. Unbelievably, the crack of semiautomatic gunfire continued. Shot after shot. All from the same place. Concentrated gunfire. Short bursts. It was as if the shooters were picking targets rather than aiming randomly. So who were they shooting at? And why weren't the cops rushing the building? He scanned the courthouse roof again. Perfect line of sight to the stadium. What hell was this? Terrorism? Lone wolf? Independence Day. Either made sense.

He had been trained to put himself in harm's way. His mental strength had been tested to the brink of endurance, and sometimes beyond, time after time. While the average person would naturally run or hide in fear when confronted with death, his reaction was to confront it. He processed fear differently.

He got to his feet and pushed through the fleeing crowds toward the courthouse.

Reznick edged past an older couple that had frozen in panic. "That way," he said, pointing. "Head that way and you'll be safe." He reached an intersection, and the scene that greeted him was horrifying. Dead police officers sprawled on the street and sidewalk, bleeding. Paramedics and fellow cops and passersby screamed for assistance.

A few cops had their weapons trained on the art deco courthouse across the street. The crack of gunfire sounded, and a bullet ricocheted off the ground.

Reznick dove behind a police car as bullets began to rain down, piercing the vehicle's bodywork and shattering the glass.

"Sir, get out of here!" a cop yelled, grabbing him by the shoulder.

Reznick knew immediately that it was cops being targeted. This was not international terrorism, which was usually aimed at mass casualties. It was targeted killings. The shooters were clearly intent on taking down uniformed officers. Was that the end goal? Or was causing chaos and distraction amid law enforcement just a precursor to the real plan?

The firing seemed to have died down. Sounds of more screaming, shouting, car alarms, and police sirens filled the humid air.

"Sir, you need to get the fuck out of here!" the cop said.

"FBI! I'm here to help!" Reznick's mind was racing. He turned and broke cover, dashing across East 161st Street. A chopper whirred overhead. More cops had fallen in the latest barrage. Quite a few were dead.

The bullets had stopped.

In the distance, Reznick saw people trying to take cover inside a diner. Under tables, cowering in corners. Some were pointing frantically up the street, not far from a side entrance to the courthouse. He turned and saw two men on the ground with rifles taking aim at the NYPD chopper. Semiautomatic fire crackled. The chopper lurched and spun out of control. A rotor blade fell off, crashing to the ground. Black smoke billowed in the air.

The chopper rotated wildly before dropping out of the sky, crushing passing cars headed down East 161st Street and bursting into flames, incinerating people fleeing from the Yankee Tavern.

Chaos in all directions.

Reznick crouched behind an SUV as flames licked the sky. A frightened young couple huddled in a vehicle outside a deli. He watched the riflemen get up from the ground and climb into a white van. It was like they were on the clock. Then he saw the vehicle reverse out of its parking space at high speed.

A brave injured cop lying on the ground fired off several shots in vain. The van accelerated down the street, leaving a scene of utter devastation in its wake: black smoke filling the azure-blue sky, a burning chopper, dead cops, and screaming families.

Reznick felt a switch flip inside him, accompanied by a surge of adrenaline. He sprinted across the street after the van. Running hard. Heart pounding. Faster. Faster.

A cop screamed from behind a cruiser, "Are you crazy? Get down!"

Reznick ran for three blocks along Walton Avenue as if his life depended on it, until he reached the intersection at 158th Street. He was standing in the middle of the road, vehicles moving all around him, as the van disappeared from sight, lost in traffic. He pulled out his gun. Fleeing motorists swerved to avoid him.

A motorcyclist slowed down.

Reznick pointed the gun at him, flashing his FBI ID, glad to have the official identification in his wallet. "Emergency!"

The motorcyclist flipped up his visor. "Fuck is going on?"

Reznick hauled the guy off the Yamaha. "Emergency!"

"Are you kidding me, man?"

Reznick got on the bike, revved it hard. He opened up the throttle and gunned the bike down Walton Avenue, heading south, away from the chaos around the stadium. The pursuit was underway. He careened through a red light and nearly crashed headlong into a truck. He accelerated hard, riding like a maniac, desperate to catch sight of the vehicle. There were traffic cameras everywhere, and he knew the cops would have a fix on the van. At least he hoped they would. But certainly, experts at the NYPD's lower Manhattan headquarters would be tracking the van's position. So where the hell was backup?

A minute later, farther up the road, Reznick thought he spotted the van, snaking through traffic.

He revved the bike to the max. He was closing in.

Up ahead, the van ran a stop sign.

Reznick swerved hard to avoid a pickup truck. Head down, he crouched behind the windshield, hanging on to the bike for dear life as he gave pursuit.

Five

The Strategic Information Operations Center (SIOC), the FBI's global command post on the fifth floor of the Hoover Building in Washington, DC, was tense. Most members of the crisis action team were watching the real-time events unfold in New York on the huge video wall. Dozens of special agents were liaising on secure phone lines with colleagues in New York and also with the FBI's Counterterrorism Center in McLean, Virginia, as they coordinated the response of law enforcement and intelligence agencies. And all the while, SIOC was sifting through the vast amount of footage and information that was pouring in from all directions as the attack developed.

FBI assistant director Martha Meyerstein stood, arms crossed, watching the motorcycle pursue the white van, the footage streaming from an NYPD surveillance drone.

"I want a close-up of the guy on the motorbike," she said. "What's taking so long? And can we get the other real-time TV news feeds—NBC, CNN, Fox—so I can get the big picture of exactly what the hell is happening?"

The other screens on the video wall filled up with live TV news feeds from outside Yankee Stadium. Police were pushing back crowds, some of them attendees who'd come for the game, and the usual gawkers drawn to any notable event. Confusion, panic, and pandemonium broke out, then settled, then broke out again. In the background, paramedics attended to the wounded officers, desperately fighting to save lives. So far, other than those killed by the falling helicopter, all the victims appeared to be police officers.

Meyerstein tried to process the crazy chain of events. The full enormity of what was happening was playing out on live TV across America. The cold-blooded killings would reverberate across not only the intelligence community but the nation as a whole. And the fact that the attack had taken place on Independence Day might very well be symbolic. The question remained: Was this a terrorist attack on the nation, like 9/11, or was this an act of domestic terrorism from an anti-government militia intent on decimating the police?

Meyerstein's gaze was drawn back to the live coverage from a news chopper tracking the pursuit and beaming it into millions of households across America. The guy on the motorcycle was still pursuing the white cargo van through the Bronx. She couldn't believe not only how reckless the pursuer was but also how courageous. He wasn't wearing a helmet or protective leather. But he was dogged in his determination to stick with the van despite the high speeds they were reaching.

A young analyst shouted across the room, "I've got a visual of the pursuer!"

"From when?"

"From two minutes and ten seconds ago. And you're not going to believe it."

"Spit it out!"

"It's Reznick! Jon Reznick is in pursuit. He's the guy on the bike."

Meyerstein turned around and looked at the analyst, who was sitting in front of a laptop. "What?!"

"That is Jon Reznick. On the bike. That's him!"

"Are you sure?"

"Positive, ma'am. We've pieced together the footage."

"Play it!"

Up on one of the big screens, the edited footage began to play.

The shooting started and the NYPD surveillance cameras outside the stadium showed Jon Reznick and his daughter taking cover. Lauren disappeared into the crowds as she ran away from the stadium. The footage then showed Reznick emerging from the fleeing crowds, running past the dead and dying cops.

Meyerstein stared up at the video wall, dumbstruck.

The footage rolled on. Reznick took cover behind a police cruiser for a few moments, then headed toward the courthouse from where the gunfire was coming. Then an NYPD surveillance camera captured Reznick hauling a poor guy off his motorcycle before beginning the high-speed chase to catch up with the sniper guys in the van.

"Facial recognition has just confirmed the match against our records, ma'am," the analyst said. "That is 100 percent Jon Reznick. But at this stage, we don't know who the young woman is that he was with."

Meyerstein said, "That's his daughter, Lauren Reznick."

The analyst keyed in the name. "I'm on it."

Meyerstein shook her head, realizing she might be about to watch Reznick get killed live on air. She began to pace the room, eyes on the live chopper feed showing Reznick virtually hanging off the motorcycle as he rocketed around a corner, risking life and limb. "He needs backup! Where's the NYPD? Where's Homeland Security? Where is the goddamn New York FBI?"

"Homeland Security agents are on the ground," the analyst shouted back. "Multiple police cars converging on this part of the Bronx; all the resources were down beside Yankee Stadium, and that's where all the carnage was."

"Damn! What about a perimeter?"

"Police are setting up a three-mile radius at this moment."

Meyerstein felt herself getting more and more agitated. "And we're having to rely on a news helicopter to cover this?"

"NYPD are getting their own helicopter up in the air as we speak."

Meyerstein shook her head. "Not good enough," she said. "Not acceptable."

Her cell phone rang.

"Martha, what the hell is happening in New York?" The voice belonged to Bill O'Donoghue, director of the FBI.

Meyerstein's heart sank. The last thing she needed was for the finger-pointing to start already. She needed to focus on the important task at hand. Besides, she was only even in the office on the Fourth because she'd wanted to catch up on a backlog of paperwork, assuming it would be a quiet day. "I am aware of the situation, sir . . ."

"Should we prepare for further attacks? Are there others out there?"

"We're exploring that possibility."

"I've just spoken to Herb Fonseca, the President's national security adviser, and he says the President wants answers. Fast."

"Herb always wants answers fast, Bill. Look, we're up to our eyes in it. Gimme an hour."

"We haven't got an hour."

"We're analyzing all the surveillance and news footage as it comes in. It could take some time to establish what exactly is going on."

"We need people on the ground. This chase is playing out on live TV."

"I'm well aware of that. I'm already in the office, watching the whole thing. Have been for the last three and a half minutes."

"Where are you exactly?"

"SIOC, fifth floor."

"I was told there's a guy pursuing the suspects on a motorcycle. Is that right?"

"Correct. And guess what? Jon Reznick is the guy in pursuit. Just got confirmation."

"What the hell? *Our* Jon Reznick?"

"Affirmative, sir."

"Shit, you've got to be kidding," O'Donoghue said.

"Where are you? I thought you were on vacation."

"I am. We're in the Hamptons, but I'm leaving my family and coming in. It's a major attack, clearly. But I'm concerned that the damage will only be compounded by Reznick."

Meyerstein bristled at the criticism. Her boss had always been wary of the ex-Delta operator and government hit man working in any capacity for the FBI. He didn't like the way Reznick crossed boundaries, unconcerned with the legality of his actions. O'Donoghue, a stickler for detail and protocol, worried about taking the fall if it were ever revealed that the FBI was allowing a former assassin to work on highly classified operations without any congressional oversight. But right now he seemed to be ignoring the big picture of the terrorist attack.

"Sir, with respect, you seem to be missing the major point that Jon Reznick is the good guy, chasing the bad guys. He is responding to this terrible incident. He's the one chasing down the snipers responsible for this massacre. He's on our goddamn side, sir."

Meyerstein was struggling to keep her anger in check.

"I keep on hearing that, Martha. But he's trouble. He attracts trouble."

"Sir, this is a serious attack on New York. That's the story, not the potential fallout if the identity of the guy who's pursuing the terrorists is revealed."

"Don't downplay how serious this could be for us within the intelligence community, Martha."

"This attack is an intelligence failure, sir. Our failure. We have to take responsibility for this."

"We also have to take responsibility for people who work for us. In particular, Jon Reznick. Everyone will be asking questions. Who is this guy? Why did he act this way? What's his background? We need to consider how this will all play out. The media will have a field day, you can bet. They'll be looking for a hero, and they will find out who he is. It's bad enough that we didn't have any inkling of this terrible attack before it happened. When the finger-pointing starts, it's going to get worse."

"Sir, with respect, we can worry about that another day. First and foremost, these guys need to be neutralized."

"What about the NYPD?" O'Donoghue cleared his throat. "Where the hell are they?"

"Sir, with respect again, today's fatalities were mostly cops. They're having to respond to this on multiple fronts. They're mustering as many units as possible, and of course field office emergency plans have been activated across the city."

"But where are the cops? It can't just be Reznick in pursuit."

"They're on the ground and in the air and are closing in. Reznick just happens to be who the news cameras are focusing on because he's closest to the snipers' vehicle."

"Goddamn, never a break. Keep me updated. I'm heading in to New York. And I want you there too, on the next plane. The shit's gonna hit the fan on this."

Six

Reznick was tearing through the Bronx streets at high speed on the bike. Down side streets, running red lights and sailing through crosswalks. He screwed up his eyes against the harsh sunlight. He felt the adrenaline coursing through his body. The van ahead veered sharply right as it headed north along Third Avenue, driving deeper and deeper into the Bronx. He hung on to the bike as he sped on, past grim skyscrapers, graffiti scrawled on walls, and metal shutters.

Reznick accelerated harder as he weaved in and out of traffic. The van sped along East Tremont Avenue, traffic flashing past.

Semi-industrial. Urban wasteland.

Reznick was so close to the van, he could smell its dirty exhaust fumes. The van made a sharp left around a corner, onto a busy shopping street. Then another sharp turn at a nail salon and down Mapes Avenue.

A young Hispanic woman wearing headphones, oblivious to the pursuit, stepped out onto the road. For a moment, Reznick was sure the van was going to run her over, but the driver swerved at the last second. Crashed headlong into a bodega, knocking over the guy standing outside, sending him flying through the air.

Reznick braked hard and jumped off the bike, taking cover at the rear of the van, where gas was already spilling out of the tank. He trained his gun on the smoking vehicle's passenger door. "FBI! Get out of the fucking car, hands up!"

Slowly, a guy wearing navy coveralls emerged from that side of the van. The tinted windows meant Reznick couldn't see who else was inside.

"Hands up!" Reznick shouted. "Let me see them!"

The guy—tattooed, white—spun around, holding a sniper rifle.

Reznick fired two shots to the chest. The guy fell to the ground, dropping the weapon onto the road. His eyes were open wide but he was dead. Rivulets of blood trickled down the asphalt incline.

Reznick trained his gun on the driver's side.

"Driver, slowly come out with your hands in the air!"

Suddenly, two shots were fired out of the dark rear windows, glass shattering.

Reznick flung himself to the ground and crawled behind a parked car. He crouched down low as another salvo of bullets was fired in his direction. Metal splintered and glass smashed all around as Reznick lay on the ground. He crawled under the car and rolled out the other side. Onlookers began to scream.

In the chaos, the driver had bolted out of the van and was now sprinting along the street, carrying the rifle.

Reznick jumped to his feet and shouted at the bystanders. "Get off the streets! Now!" He ran over to the motorcycle, lifted it upright, and switched on the ignition. Nothing. He tried again. And again. He looked at the engine and saw a hole. A bullet had ricocheted and ripped it open. "Goddamn!"

He dropped the bike and set off on foot, giving chase.

The gunman, also wearing coveralls, was already more than one hundred yards away. He sprinted hard down the sidewalk, past frightened shop owners looking to see what had happened.

He crossed the road as a Jeep swerved to avoid him. The rifleman disappeared down a side street. Reznick's heart was hammering as he turned the corner. He knew the importance of capturing the second sniper alive. The guy could be brought in and interrogated by police: What was their motivation? Were there others out there? The driver ran down into a subway station, disappearing from sight.

Reznick bounded down the steps, barging past emerging passengers. "Out of the goddamn way!"

People jumped for cover.

Reznick was taking two steps at a time. At the bottom, he turned right, gun in hand. A handful of passengers ducked for cover, but one young woman pointed the other way.

"Look out!"

Reznick spun around, hitting the concrete floor. The guy stood close to the turnstiles, about to shoot into the crowded station. Reznick drilled two shots into the man's forehead. The rifle fell from his hands.

Screams echoed through the station. Passengers on the platform stared in horror.

Reznick ran forward, kicked the rifle out of the man's reach, gun still trained on the motionless body.

The man's eyes were open, but blood was already congealing around his head.

Seven

The cops descended the subway stairs en masse, guns drawn.

A burly black NYPD officer trained his gun on Reznick. "Freeze! Drop the fucking gun!"

Reznick did as he was told.

"Hands on head!"

Reznick complied.

The cop had him covered. "Just stay right there," he said. "Do not make a move."

A couple of cops approached from the sides, pulled his arms back, and cuffed his wrists extra tight, as if to make a point.

Reznick watched the cops approach the dead sniper. Blood still oozed out of the head wounds, onto the ground.

A cop's radio crackled to life. "Got him. He's here. The perp is dead."

Reznick said, "The dead guy was one of the shooters. He was driving the van. I got the other guy outside a bodega."

The cop said, "Yeah?" He spoke again into his radio. "The guy who's cuffed said he got both of them. Yeah, I'm telling you that's what he's saying."

Reznick said, "You want to get these cuffs off?"

The cop said, "What's your name?"

Reznick said, "Back pocket has my ID and whatever you need."

The cop rifled in the back pocket of his jeans and pulled out his wallet. He scanned the driver's license and the FBI ID. "Rockland, Maine. Long way from home. What are you in New York for?"

"Yankees game."

"It says here you're FBI. Is this fake?"

Reznick winced from the cuffs biting into his wrists. "No, it's not fake. You mind getting me the hell out of these?"

The cop signaled a couple of his colleagues over. He frisked Reznick. "You shouldn't be carrying in New York City," he said.

"I've got special authorization."

"Yeah? Then where's your concealed carry permit?"

Reznick stared at the cop. "Listen very carefully. I'm authorized by the assistant director of the FBI, Martha Meyerstein. Why don't you call her?"

A fresh-faced young cop chewing gum said, "Assistant director, huh? Were you involved in the attack? Are you covering your ass, silencing your partners? Is that what happened?"

Reznick fixed his gaze on the kid. "There are dead police officers outside Yankee Stadium . . ."

The young cop stepped forward, eyeballing Reznick. "You don't have to tell us that, smart-ass."

"Are you serious? You're giving *me* a hard time? The guy that chased after the fuckers and took them down? Seriously?"

The black cop signaled for the younger hothead cop to get out of Reznick's face.

A few long minutes later, four detectives wearing shirts and ties arrived.

Reznick was hauled back up the stairs, into the back of a car, then, because police in the Bronx were overwhelmed, driven all the way down to an NYPD precinct in lower Manhattan.

There was an overwhelming sense of burning rage from the police. The detectives as well as the uniformed cops in the precinct. Reznick could see it in their eyes. He understood why. Their fellow cops had been mowed down in cold blood. While millions of Americans would be celebrating their country's independence on the Fourth of July, enjoying steaks and ribs at barbecues, drinks, and parades and baseball on TV, the NYPD was mourning the loss of some of their finest. Officers killed in the line of duty. He knew cops. And they would be hell-bent on avenging the fallen officers, come what may. The anger and frustration could so easily boil over.

It was easy to see why. Officers not returning home to their families. The dreaded knock at the door with the terrible news. Then the days and weeks of funerals and mourning. The killings would reverberate for years in New York and across America. And each and every Fourth of July, the NYPD would be reminded of one of their darkest days.

Why wouldn't they be angry? But he also knew it was a volatile situation. And he needed to be careful how he approached the whole thing.

A cop unshackled his hands for a moment and cuffed his wrists at his front, making him marginally more comfortable. "That OK?"

Reznick nodded and followed a couple of mean-looking cops down a corridor until they got to a windowless room. Inside, two detectives wearing dress shirts and clip-on ties were sitting behind a desk. Notepad, four small bottles of water, and their cell phones in front of them. A fan in the corner.

The detectives nodded. One pointed to the chair opposite.

Reznick sat down and sighed. His head was swimming. He thought of Lauren and prayed she had gotten to safety. She was smart. And tough.

One of the detectives pushed a bottle of water toward him. "Drink it," he said.

Reznick picked up the bottle of water with both hands and took a couple of gulps. It felt good.

"You OK?" one said.

Reznick shrugged. "As well as could be expected after everything that happened."

The younger of the two detectives took off his jacket and draped it over the back of his seat. His colleague started the recording machine and checked his watch. "It's 11:58 a.m., July fourth." He looked across the table at Reznick. "We're trying to establish a few facts. I'm sure you understand. Let's get a few basics down. Clear?"

"Crystal."

"What is your name?"

Reznick sighed. "I think you know my name."

"I'll ask you again. What is your name?"

"My name is Jon Reznick."

The detective scribbled down the details. "That's better. And what do you do?"

Reznick sighed.

"Your ID says you're a special agent with the FBI. Is that true?"

"I work as a consultant for the FBI. That's probably a more accurate assessment. I'm not a special agent in the traditional sense."

The detectives shared a dubious look. "A consultant?" the younger detective said.

"Yes."

He scowled. "What the hell does that mean? I've never in my life heard of a special agent who was a consultant."

Reznick shrugged. "It's a special relationship I have with the FBI."

"And what does this special relationship entail?"

"It's like an advisory role, as and when required."

"As and when required . . . Do you want to help us out here, Jon? What does that mean?"

"It means sometimes I'm called in on investigations which involve national security, as an example."

"So you're an FBI consultant who advises on national security, *for example*, and you just happened to be up by Yankee Stadium when this whole shitstorm happened?"

"That is correct."

"And that was just pure coincidence."

Reznick knew from the detective's tone of voice that he didn't believe a word of his story. "My being there this morning had nothing to do with my work, if that's what you're getting at. I was with my daughter. Lauren Reznick. College student."

The older detective shook his head. "Jon, I'm going to be honest with you. I'm not buying this story. Doesn't ring true."

"Look, I understand why the NYPD hauled me in. I get it. If I was in your shoes, I would take the same approach. You don't know me. And I was there when this happened. But I believe you're wasting precious time focusing your efforts on me. This is not about me. We don't even know if the attacks are over. What if the attack at the stadium is only part of something larger planned for the city?"

"We'll focus on whoever we wish to focus on. And we'll be the judge of your honesty, or not. Are we clear, Mr. Reznick?"

Reznick shifted in his seat, feeling the malevolent gaze of both detectives. "I'm asking you to speak to the FBI. They know me. A quick call, and this can all be ironed out."

"Who were you with?"

"What do you mean, who was I with?"

"Simple question, Jon," said the older detective. "We've got all the time in the world. Who did you attend the game with?"

"I was with my daughter, Lauren Reznick. Haven't you checked the surveillance footage from outside the stadium?"

The younger cop sighed. "We'll ask the questions, Mr. Reznick. Tell me about Lauren. Where is she now?"

"I have no idea."

"Why not?"

"It all went to shit after the shooting started. I told her to get the hell away from the stadium. We stopped a cab and she got in. Hopefully she's safe and sound back at our hotel."

"What's the name of the hotel?"

"The Pierre."

The detective whistled and leaned back in his seat. "That's a nice place." He turned to his colleague. "How many FBI agents you know can afford to hang out there on their salaries?"

"I'm a consultant. I have savings."

"Lucky you. Have you always worked for the FBI, Mr. Reznick?"

Reznick could see that the interrogation was already headed south. He could see they were wasting time, his and theirs. He felt frustrated. "Four years. I'm not exactly sure about the dates. Listen, you need to find out who the guys were who carried out the killings."

"'Not exactly sure about the dates,'" he parroted. The tone of the man's voice insinuated that Reznick was lying. "Where are you from, Mr. Reznick?"

"Rockland, Maine."

"You like baseball?"

Reznick felt increasingly frustrated at the line of questioning. He shook his head. "What the hell kind of question is that? What does that mean?"

"It means, do you like baseball? A simple question. You seem to be having trouble answering simple questions. Why is that? Would you like to answer it?"

"Yeah, I like baseball. Happy?"

"And your daughter lives in New York?"

Reznick nodded. "Just for the summer. She's an intern."

"Where?"

Reznick gave the address of the apartment in Lenox Hill where she was sharing a room and the name of the publishing company where she was interning. "Look, I would appreciate it if I could call her. To see if she's back home or back at the hotel."

"You'll have a chance to call her. Just not now. You know, I've been doing this job for a long, long time. And you get to understand people. Their motivations. Their moods."

Reznick sighed. "What is this, amateur psychologist hour?"

"Very funny. I've got to say, you seem very blasé, despite being caught up in this massacre and having just killed two men."

"Blasé? Are you kidding me? It's not me that's blasé. I'm worried about my daughter. I don't know where she is. I'm also worried this might not be an isolated incident. Did the shooters have help? Is someone pulling the strings? Why aren't you trying to find out more about the two guys who did it?"

"We are, don't worry. But we're focusing right now on establishing exactly who you are and how you got caught up in all this. The shots that killed the two alleged snipers were very precise. You military, Mr. Reznick?"

"I'd rather not talk too much about that."

The detective leaned forward, hands clasped. "That's interesting too, Mr. Reznick."

"If you insist."

"Listen, smart-ass, we have New York officers lying dead up in the Bronx. We want answers. And you will not leave here until you give us those answers."

"This is unbelievable. Check the footage, I took those guys down."

"I asked you a question. So I'm going to ask it again. And I'll ask it until I get a real answer. Are you ex-military? Special Forces?"

Reznick said nothing. He wasn't going to get dragged into answering questions about his military past, whether Delta or his work for the government. Besides, most of it was classified.

"Alright. Where did you learn to shoot like that?"

31

Reznick sighed.

"You taking the Fifth, Jon?"

"No, I'm not taking the Fifth."

"Let me get this straight, Jon. You were with your daughter, waiting to go into a Yankees game. There was shooting. And you decided to commandeer a motorcycle and chase after those two guys, despite them being heavily armed? Is that really your story?"

"Yeah, that's right."

"Why?"

"Why what?"

The older detective flushed with anger. "Don't get smart. We lost eight cops today. Eight of our finest."

"Listen, I should know. I saw the whole thing unfold. I saw those officers. Have you been up there and seen the mess? The blood? The bodies?"

The younger detective scribbled some notes. "Why did you give chase? I don't think most special agents would react the way you did. I think they would call in help. Maybe call 911. Then request an NYPD Emergency Service Unit to hunt down the guys. No way would they do it single-handed."

"I'm going to give you a name. You need to call Martha Meyerstein, assistant director of the FBI in DC. She knows me very well. I work directly with her."

The younger detective scribbled the name as his colleague scrutinized Reznick's demeanor, as if looking for signs of deception.

"Meyerstein," Reznick repeated. "Are you telling me you haven't even verified my ID yet?"

"We're looking into that, trust me."

The older detective said, "Jon, my name's Detective Francis Sheerin."

Reznick nodded.

"I'm going to be up-front with you and tell you where we're at . . . I'm wondering . . . were you working on an undercover operation for the FBI up in the Bronx this morning?"

Reznick shook his head. "Oh, I get it. You're trying to implicate me and the FBI, as if this was in some way related to an investigation gone wrong, am I right?"

"Answer the question," Sheerin said. "Were you on an undercover FBI operation in the Bronx this morning?"

"No, I was not."

Sheerin folded his arms, unimpressed. "So you're telling me that these guys who began firing were not known to the FBI?"

"I have no idea if they were known to the FBI. But I can categorically tell you that this wasn't an FBI operation. I was with my daughter. I'm in New York solely for a personal vacation."

"And you came armed with a gun and just so happened to be directly outside Yankee Stadium when the snipers attacked? The whole thing doesn't add up. Do you understand that?"

"You've got this all wrong. My daughter is living in New York for the summer. She's a student, Bennington."

"Vermont is a long way from New York, Mr. Reznick."

Reznick sighed. "She has an internship at a publishing company. I think I already mentioned that."

Sheerin leaned over and whispered in his colleague's ear before addressing Reznick again. "We're going to take a break for a few minutes. We'll continue this interview when we return."

The detectives got up, picked up their notes, and left the room.

Reznick stretched his legs and arms the best he could, shifting in his seat as he waited. Twenty minutes later, the detectives returned and resumed the interview.

Sheerin leaned forward. "Seems like the FBI does know you."

"That's good. Are you going to let me go?"

Sheerin smiled, his face inches from Reznick's. "What do you think?"

"I think you're going to keep me here until you're satisfied that my story is correct."

"Right on the money, Jon. Tell me, what kind of operation was the FBI running? You can understand that we need to know that, can't you?"

Reznick sighed. "Listen, I thought I explained this. I was attending a ball game with my daughter. Man, this is just laughable."

"This is no joke. I'm sure you must be only too aware how police respond when their colleagues get murdered. They get angry. Very, very angry. I've got to say, the mood inside this precinct is, frankly, incendiary."

"I'm not surprised. Listen, I already told you, I was not involved in any operation. To my knowledge, there was no FBI operation."

"Well, we don't believe you."

Reznick could see it was going to be a long, long day.

"You see, here's another thing. I've been checking with some of my own sources. And the two snipers were known to both the NYPD and the FBI. Bit of a coincidence, don't you think?"

"I have no idea who the shooters were, I'm telling you. I will swear in a court of law, on the Bible, I wasn't on an FBI operation. I was with my daughter, going to watch the Yankees on the Fourth of July. Check the footage. What sort of operation is carried out with someone's daughter along?"

Sheerin rolled up his sleeves and leaned back in his seat. "We have the blood of dead cops running in the streets of the Bronx. Don't tell me you didn't know anything about these guys. You're insulting my intelligence."

The atmosphere in the interview room was suddenly incredibly charged. The tension palpable.

"Listen, you might want to check with an NYPD detective I know. Detective Acosta, Nineteenth Precinct. Upper East Side. A year ago my daughter was a victim of a hit-and-run that put her in a coma. Acosta will vouch for me."

The younger detective scribbled down the details as Reznick sketched out the story of the corrupt diplomat who'd knocked down his daughter while speeding through the streets of New York last year. He'd ended up working alongside the FBI and the NYPD to bring the diplomat and his illegal activities to a halt.

Sheerin stared at him long and hard. "Seems like trouble just follows you around when you're in New York, Jon. Why is that?"

"Sometimes, that's just the way it is."

Eventually, the interview ended for a second time and Reznick was escorted, still handcuffed, to the bathroom. He returned to the interview room, a fresh bottle of water at his side of the desk. He opened it up and took a drink. The cold water felt good; on such a blazing hot day, even the air-conditioning inside the precinct building couldn't keep up. He sat back down in his seat.

They left him there for hours.

He was given a sandwich. A couple of coffees. The detectives finally returned just after three p.m. This time, they were accompanied by Special Agent Leon Cortez from the New York field office.

"Hey, Jon, you OK?" Cortez asked.

Reznick was glad to see him again. He remembered Cortez from the previous summer. The special agent exuded a certain confidence, although his eyes seemed a bit bloodshot now, as if from lack of sleep. But he looked sharp in his well-cut navy suit, white shirt, pale-blue tie, and shiny black shoes.

Reznick nodded. "I'm fine. You want to get me out of here? I'm done."

Just before four p.m., Reznick was released by the NYPD into the custody of the FBI. He was taken directly to the FBI's New York office in lower Manhattan and up to the twenty-sixth floor and into the conference room. Martha Meyerstein was sitting on the edge of a desk, arms folded. The big screens behind her were showing spectator cell phone footage from outside the stadium as the sniper attacks erupted.

"What the hell took you guys so long getting me out of there?" Reznick asked.

Meyerstein pointed to the screens. "Eight NYPD officers dead. That's what. They're on the warpath. And the fact that you got right in the middle of everything has heightened their suspicions that there was a connection. They're pissed, Jon."

"Yeah, well, so am I. Having to sit and listen to those guys grilling me as if I was involved in some FBI operation up in the Bronx."

"Look at it from their point of view. It doesn't look good. And while we appreciate you risking your life to go after these guys, we've been forced into damage-control mode with both the police and the media. No one wants to believe that you're just a John McClane good guy in the right place at the right time."

"I need to find out if Lauren is OK. I need to call her."

"Go right ahead," Meyerstein said.

Reznick headed over to the window and called his daughter's cell phone. He stared out over the lower Manhattan skyscrapers as he waited for it to ring. It had been nearly five hours since the attack. And he was worried sick for her.

Lauren's cell phone rang six times before voice mail picked up.

Reznick left a message, asking for her to call and confirm she was OK.

Meyerstein said, "No luck?"

Reznick shook his head.

"She'll be fine, Jon. She's a tough, smart girl. I'm sure she got out of there."

Reznick wondered if he had made the wrong call. Should he have stayed with his daughter instead of going after the snipers?

As if reading his mind, Meyerstein said, "It was great work getting those guys. Really great."

Reznick's gaze was drawn to the huge screens showing the two white guys he had taken out. The shooters. He stared long and hard at the close-ups showing heavily tattooed forearms and necks and dead blue eyes on both. "Is that them?"

Meyerstein nodded.

"What do we know about them?"

"Interesting crew. These are the O'Keefe brothers. The guy on the right, Travis, age twenty-four, was the guy you killed outside the bodega. The guy on the left, Ryan, age twenty-five, was the one killed on the subway platform."

"Where are they from?"

"Upstate New York, originally. We have a previous address, a walk-up in the East Village, few months back. But they've served serious time over the years."

Reznick ran his hands across his face. "So what's the motivation? Are we talking far-right anti-government nuts? Militia?"

"Maybe. The O'Keefes are serious methamphetamine dealers. Very dangerous. They're linked to the Aryan Circle."

"Who the hell are they?"

"It's a prison gang that broke away from the Aryan Brotherhood. Aryan Circle also believes in race purity, white supremacist ideology, but they're far more dogmatic about it."

"Sounds like a nice crowd."

"Back in 2007, some of their guys were responsible for killing two police officers down in Louisiana."

"So these O'Keefe brothers have done time. For what?"

"Take your pick. Methamphetamine dealing, knife fights in jail. Nasty pair. Also did time for stealing a trailer full of guns. Got out three months back. We believe they were targeted for recruitment by Aryan Circle leaders because they were only in for six and seven years respectively, which meant that when they got out, they could carry out whatever it is the leadership wants carried out."

"What's the motivation? Eight police officers dead. Why?"

"As I said, the group they are associated with has history. Gang experts are working on this as we speak. The officers killed today were white, Hispanic, and black. So they didn't discriminate in that sense. Whatever motivated this, it transcends their race-hate message. That's something we'll look closer at in the coming hours and days."

"Have they been on the FBI's radar at all?"

Meyerstein cleared her throat and shrugged, as if she didn't yet know the full facts herself. "We had a task force looking into their activities."

"The cops seemed to think the FBI knew about these guys. You're not holding back something, are you, Martha?"

"We're trying to find out more about that and exactly how much we knew about them."

Reznick thought her answer sounded defensive. Not like her.

"They're not on a watch list or anything, if that's what you're getting at."

Reznick looked at the screens and shook his head. "What else do you know about these two—family, personal lives . . . ?"

"Mother still lives upstate. Alcoholic. Father abandoned them when they were young. Brought up ostensibly by their stepfather."

"And where's he?"

Meyerstein sighed. "You're asking a lot of questions, Jon."

Reznick looked at her. "Martha, am I missing something? Is there a problem?"

"No, no problem."

"So tell me about the stepfather."

Meyerstein shifted on the desk. "The stepfather is dead."

"When did he die? How did he die?"

She looked away, seeming irritated by the questions. Her gaze wandered around the room for a few moments. Finally, she said, "He died about three months ago."

"Three months ago? So, I'm just guessing here, but if the attack didn't seem to be about race, is this stepfather's death connected in some way to the actions of these two crazies? Have they been triggered in some way by it?"

Meyerstein shrugged. "We're getting off base. We don't know what the motivation for this was. The fact remains that they were members of a neo-Nazi prison gang that has been linked in the past to the murders of police officers. Those are the facts."

She sounded more abrasive and impatient than he'd ever heard her, as if she didn't want to reveal the full extent of her knowledge. Reznick wasn't offended. He didn't think her caginess was anything to do with him personally. But he was curious. "What about their associates?"

"We're working on that. They didn't have wives, steady girlfriends, that kind of thing. Constantly on the move. There's an older brother on Long Island."

"What does he know about it?"

"He's the smart one in the family. He got out and went to college. Got a good job working as a stock market analyst in Manhattan."

Reznick contemplated the information. The brother might not know anything, but they needed to question him.

"So that's three brothers," Meyerstein continued. "A smart one who got the hell out when he could. And the two crazies you killed today. But there's a fourth brother."

Reznick shrugged. "What about him?"

"The fourth brother, the youngest, is the one giving us real cause for concern. We're trying to trace him. So far without success."

"And what do we know about the fourth brother?"

Meyerstein shook her head. "Todd O'Keefe. Hard-core Aryan Brotherhood." She picked up a remote control, pressed a couple of buttons. A mug shot appeared on the big screen beside a photo of a tattooed torso. Inked swastikas adorned the side of the guy's neck, and an Irish shamrock and swastika spread across his chest.

"This guy looks like a handful."

"He's hyper-violent. And as luck would have it, he was also released from Leavenworth three months ago, two days after his brothers. Crazy coincidence, I think."

"Yeah, so where the hell is he?"

"That's the problem. We don't know."

Reznick contemplated the situation. "I want to speak to the brother we do know about."

"Out on Long Island?"

"Any objection to me asking him some questions?"

"That can be arranged."

Eight

Todd O'Keefe splashed cold water on his face and ran his fingers through his scraggly beard as he hunkered down in a run-down New Jersey motel. The curtains were already drawn, blocking out the late-afternoon sun. The room was bathed in a pale-yellow light. But it might as well have been the dead of night.

He put on headphones, switched on a Ted Nugent playlist on his iPhone, and got down on the floor where he began a punishing work-out, starting with push-ups.

He felt a black anger beginning to consume his soul. His brothers were dead. His flesh and blood. He hadn't envisioned it ending like that. He closed his eyes for a second. His mind flashed to a photo of Travis and Ryan as kids, arms wrapped protectively around their baby brother. The three amigos, they liked to call themselves.

O'Keefe felt his muscles tighten as he continued the push-ups. He felt himself working up a sweat. The endorphins began to kick in. The blood was flowing. The sound of heavy guitar riffs was hyping him up for what lay ahead. But he didn't feel as euphoric as he usually did during his physical exercises. He felt homicidal.

The news images of his brothers' bodies covered by police sheets, lying in separate locations in New York City, burned into his psyche. Like a branding iron.

He tried to erase the image from his mind. He didn't want to imagine their final moments. He would find out who was responsible. And he would avenge them. But at that moment, he wanted to remember them as they were. Warriors. Tough guys. Blood brothers.

As he continued his push-ups, O'Keefe reveled in the exertion. His muscles being stretched to the max. As his limbs began to ache, he relished the pain. Pain was good. Pain would set him free.

One hundred. Two hundred. Three hundred. When he began the sit-ups, he did two hundred straight, without stopping. His stomach muscles tightened. He felt ripped. His breathing edged up a notch. And then another, and another, the more he pushed himself.

His watch's alarm beeped, signaling that his thirty minutes of exercise time was up. No breaks. No letup. The way he liked it. The way he had trained in the yard back at Leavenworth. He had kept up the same fitness regimen on the outside. Up at dawn, running, punching bags, then heading to the gym. Sweating. Fighting. That's what he did.

O'Keefe sat up, cross-legged on the floor, back leaning against the bed. He reached over to his jeans and took his cell phone out of his pocket. He checked his messages. Still nothing. He switched off the music. Then he closed his eyes and began to meditate.

He imagined a river. A cold river. And it flowed on through a beautiful meadow. He felt himself drifting off. Escaping in his mind. He felt himself walking down an alpine path, surveying the wildflowers and grass and fields. The smell of pine and moss lingered in his senses. When he was done, he felt mentally cleansed. His soul was free again.

He began to order his thoughts.

Meditation was something he had scoffed at when he had first entered the prison system. It wasn't for the likes of him, he thought. He'd always considered meditation and yoga to be the habit of nuts in California. He began to change his mind when he saw a fellow inmate, a man he trusted, feared even, meditating as he sat in his cell. The man had told O'Keefe that he could escape the confines of his incarceration when he meditated. He could move wherever he wanted in his mind. He was free. No one could touch him. And it was true.

The man had turned O'Keefe on to weights. Tough weights. Lifting weights he couldn't ever imagine lifting or shifting. But he did. The man was like a surrogate father to him inside. He seemed to sense O'Keefe's mood swings. It was almost like the man had a sixth sense that allowed him to know what to say or do in any given moment.

O'Keefe studied how the man carried himself in Leavenworth. The conditions, especially in summer, were extreme. The prison was known as "the hot house" because of the small, sweltering cells. He watched the way the man, who led the Brand in Leavenworth, ruled over the prisoners like a god. The fearsome crew surrounding the man fascinated O'Keefe. He wanted to be like them. All he had to do was make his mark, show that he could be taken seriously. That he would back up fellow brothers in the yard or outside. All he had to do was kill a Mexican or black inmate.

He killed one of each. Those who were supposed to witness it did. Those who weren't supposed to turned a blind eye. That was the way it worked on the inside.

O'Keefe was in. He got the essential shamrock tattooed in the middle of his chest, alongside a swastika. He reveled in the reactions of other inmates. No one fucked with him anymore. The man he revered, who was on the ruling three-man Aryan Brotherhood Commission, showed him the ropes. How they ran the heroin in and out of the yard. Even the inmates in solitary were on H. It was all around. But the man didn't touch it, so neither did O'Keefe. He focused on physical toughness. Grueling weight sessions in the yard. Martial arts techniques. His physique began to change. He began to bulk up. And he began to take steroids. He could lift heavier and heavier weights. But it was also like throwing kerosene on a fire: it ignited his latent rage.

O'Keefe began to grow in influence among the Brotherhood. He was increasingly trusted. He began to organize the drug mules. Crooked guards, bent lawyers, prison visitors. Heroin, meth, marijuana, pills, cocaine. Swallowed in balloons or condoms. Instructions were sent out through coded messages via ordinary mail, bribed prison staff, or even inmates' visitors. There was always a way. The money rolled in.

O'Keefe began to realize that while the Brotherhood still touted its white supremacy, that ideology had been subjugated in favor of its enterprises. Drug dealing. Protection money.

The more he got to know the man, the more he grew to respect him. The man was six foot seven, brawny, and strangely charismatic. Like all the top AB guys, he was well read in Nietzsche, Sun Tzu, Machiavelli, and Tolkien, among others. The man's personal favorite was *Mein Kampf*.

The bond between O'Keefe and the man became even stronger.

Not long after, the man revealed that he wasn't just a member of the Commission. He was the shot caller. The guy at the top who gave orders. The rules were simple: you followed the orders to the letter, or you were killed. O'Keefe knew that. And when he was released after serving his sentence, he knew how it worked. He was given orders, he carried them out.

But his orders for today, Independence Day, were more than just orders to carry out. This mission was also deeply personal.

After his release, O'Keefe had talked at length with his brothers about avenging the death of Charlie Campbell. About meting out justice. They had talked of finding the cop who'd put him in the choke hold that had killed him and making him die a slow death in the same way. But those plans were cast aside when the man sent a coded hand-written message.

It was delivered to a PO box near Ithaca. O'Keefe picked it up and deciphered the contents. He'd offered the job to Travis and Ryan as a gift, a way of demonstrating to the man that his brothers were as worthy as he was.

O'Keefe felt devastated his brothers had died. He was partly responsible. But the reality was that all three of them had wanted to exact the same kind of blood justice in the name of Charlie Campbell. And all three knew there was a risk of getting killed if they carried out the attacks. Either that or being incarcerated until they died.

His cell phone rang, snapping him out of his thoughts. O'Keefe didn't recognize the caller ID. Which could only mean one thing: it was the man. He switched on the radio, playing some Eagles song, and turned up the volume to mask the sound of his voice from anyone in the room next door or outside.

"Todd, how are you holding up?"

"I've been better."

A deep sigh. "I'm sorry about your brothers, man. Really, I am."

"I know. But they knew what they were getting into. They took eight down, I heard."

"The rest of them will soon get the message, bro. Don't ever fuck with our crew. I know you'll give them an extra reminder this afternoon."

"They don't know who they're dealing with."

"They will tonight. I know who you are. I've looked into your eyes, Todd, and I can tell exactly the type of warrior you are. I know you won't let us down. And I sure as hell know you won't let Charlie's memory down. Or your brothers', God rest their souls."

O'Keefe took a deep breath. "Amen to that. Tell me, where's my ride?"

"That's why I'm calling. Cab will be out front in two minutes. We'll need to bounce you around for a little while, to make sure no one is tailing you."

"I understand."

"Anyway, get in the cab. Once the driver is confident it's clear, he'll take you to a friendly port of call. Use it as your base camp for a little while. They're expecting you."

The Hell's Angels clubhouse in Newark, New Jersey, was located on a seedy street in a run-down part of town. Inside was a bartender, a Black Sabbath song playing on the jukebox, and Fox News on the TV—a reporter standing outside Yankee Stadium—volume off.

O'Keefe pulled up a stool. The bartender placed a cold bottle of beer on the grimy wooden bar. O'Keefe took a couple of gulps. It felt good.

The jukebox began vibrating to a Metallica track. The music brought back memories. Charlie had introduced him and his brothers to all his favorite bands: Black Sabbath, Deep Purple, Led Zeppelin, Aerosmith, Ted Nugent, Stevie Ray Vaughan. Old-school.

He let his mind wander deeper and deeper into childhood memories. They'd been the toughest kids in their rural upstate neighborhood, bar none. As the youngest, he had always looked up to his two older brothers. Nothing seemed to bother them. He always admired the way they never lost face by backing down in a fight. Even when they knew they would get hammered by a group of older kids, they still faced the fuckers down. Eventually, when they grew up to be fearsome men, O'Keefe noticed the looks on other people's faces. They were scared. And that was before his two older brothers really got started.

O'Keefe's gaze was drawn to the TV. Footage of the dead NYPD officers. Goddamn it. Travis and Ryan should be here with him, sharing a toast. It wasn't fair.

He knocked back the beer. The biker behind the bar handed him another cold Heineken. "I was told that if you need anything, just to get you whatever it is."

O'Keefe stared at the guy, took a gulp of the cold beer. "I'm going to need a ride into the city."

"Not a problem. When?"

"Very soon. Got business to attend to."

The biker nodded and glanced up at the TV. "Sure thing. Well, just let me know, and I'll get you into the city, whenever you want."

O'Keefe nodded. His cell phone rang. It was the shot caller again. "You find the place OK?"

"Got it."

"Enjoy the beer. What I'd give for a cold one. Todd, I know you loved your brothers. I loved them too. We all did. And they're going to go down in AB history. But we know the risks. This is what we do. And those cops . . . well, they had it coming. What they did to Charlie and all . . ."

"I want to hit back at them."

"I know, bro. We want more blood. We demand more blood."

The line went dead.

Nine

The chopper carrying Reznick and the special agent who was playing his babysitter, Joe Farrelly, touched down on a ball field in Southampton, Long Island. Without so many words, Reznick had gotten the message: Farrelly would be Meyerstein's eyes and ears while Reznick talked to Robert O'Keefe. He was starting to wonder if he shouldn't have just left this task to others and gone to meet up with Lauren and make sure she was safe despite not returning his call.

But the more Reznick thought about it, the more he began to wonder if, just like America had learned in the weeks, months, and years after 9/11, there was more to this morning's attack. He considered it inconceivable that the FBI or even the NYPD hadn't had an inkling or a tip-off that something was coming, especially something carried out by such a well-known group. It just didn't make sense.

From Reznick's point of view, there were more questions than answers. He sat in silence, mulling them, while he and Farrelly were picked up and driven in an SUV to the oceanfront home of Robert O'Keefe.

Reznick surveyed the house—a grand Colonial mansion—as the car headed up a gravel drive fringed by beautiful oak trees.

He could see that the eldest O'Keefe brother had done phenomenally well. On the chopper he'd read the file the FBI had hastily compiled. Robert O'Keefe was the smartest of the four sons. He'd excelled at school, teachers describing him as "incredibly bright." Thanks to nearly perfect SAT scores, he'd won a merit scholarship to Cornell and become the first in his dirt-poor family to attend college. He studied economics, graduating at the top of his class, before he was snapped up by a blue-chip New York hedge fund.

The file painted a picture of the American Dream. The poor kid who rises from a humble background because of his hard work and natural, God-given talents.

Robert O'Keefe had already been interviewed by the FBI and the NYPD earlier that afternoon. But the more Reznick learned about him, the more he wanted to speak to him face-to-face, to try to understand if there was something, anything, that the FBI or the cops had overlooked or hadn't thought important.

The guy had impeccable taste. It was a beautiful house overlooking the ocean. Reznick reckoned it would have cost millions. Maybe tens of millions.

O'Keefe's wife opened the door and let them in. She wore a cream cotton sleeveless summer dress with espadrilles. Her eyes were heavy, mascara smudged. "Robert is out back," she said. "Go easy on him, please. He's pretty upset about all this."

Reznick and Farrelly followed Mrs. O'Keefe down a highly polished hallway. Professional portrait photographs of O'Keefe's kids lined the wall. The two men headed through a huge open-plan kitchen and out French doors into the garden.

O'Keefe was slumped in a wicker chair, whiskey in hand, tears running down his face. He wore a pale-blue polo shirt, jeans, and flip-flops. "Jesus Christ, I thought I was done. I answered all your questions. The other guys said they had no more questions."

Farrelly said, "I know this is a difficult situation, Mr. O'Keefe, and I know you've already given a statement to the police and my colleagues earlier today."

O'Keefe nodded. "I'm as appalled as everyone else. I'm sickened. But I didn't know anything about any of this, I swear."

Farrelly pulled up a seat beside him. "Robert, Special Agent Reznick would like to ask some particular questions. Would that be OK?"

O'Keefe sighed. "What's there to talk about? My brothers are nutcases. What more do you need to know? I'm disgusted that I came from the same gene pool."

Reznick said, "We understand. I can only imagine how painful this must've been for you."

O'Keefe cleared his throat. "It brought back a lot of the things I've been working through with my therapist. It's taken years to get my head in shape. But it's all fucking exploded today. I'm in pieces."

"I can see that," Reznick said. "And I know talking about this for the second time today is not pleasant for you. But we could really use your help to be sure we're not missing anything."

O'Keefe's eyes filled with tears. "I was just watching some of the news footage from Yankee Stadium. It's sickening. Cops? I've got friends in the NYPD. Good people."

"I know. So, do you mind answering some questions?"

O'Keefe closed his eyes for a moment as if steeling himself for the ordeal. "What do you need to know?"

Reznick turned to Farrelly. "Joe, I need a favor. Do you mind if I speak alone with Mr. O'Keefe?"

Farrelly frowned. "That's not how this was supposed to work."

"Look, I want to talk privately with Robert. If you have a problem with that, why don't you call Assistant Director Meyerstein and see if she's OK with it."

Farrelly scratched his head and grimaced before saying, "I was supposed to accompany you."

"And you did accompany me. And now I need some time alone with Mr. O'Keefe here. Call Meyerstein if you need to."

Farrelly shrugged. "Fine."

O'Keefe's wife ushered Farrelly inside.

Reznick waited until Farrelly was in the kitchen with O'Keefe's wife, out of earshot. He pulled up a seat opposite the man and sat down. He studied the face of the eldest O'Keefe. The guy resembled his crazy brothers, but without the tattoos and mean eyes. "Tough day for everyone, Robert. I'm sorry about this. I know you have nothing to do with this."

O'Keefe was shaking his head, eyes downcast, hands trembling. "I appreciate that. The guys that were here earlier bulldozed in, acting as if I was part of my brothers' crew. It's absurd. I'm telling you, I'm as freaked out as everyone else."

O'Keefe closed his eyes for a few moments as if struggling to come to terms with all of it.

"Helluva shock you must've had," Reznick said. "I can only imagine what you're going through. I don't have any brothers."

"Trust me, you don't want brothers like mine."

"You work in Manhattan, Robert?"

"General Motors Building, Fifth Avenue. Right in the heart of the city. I have an apartment where I stay during the week."

"Where's that?"

"Couple of blocks away on Lexington. Jesus, I was even supposed to be at the Yankee game today, but I had some paperwork to catch up on."

"Yankee fan, huh?"

"Yeah, since I was a kid."

"I was up there at Yankee Stadium this morning, with my daughter. We got caught up in it. We were going to the game."

O'Keefe ran his hands through his hair. "You kidding me?"

"Just going to a baseball game on the Fourth."

O'Keefe nodded. "Things like this aren't supposed to happen. You read about shit like this. I can't begin to imagine what went on there."

"It was rough. Robert, I believe that something like this, what happened today, carried out by two of your brothers, couldn't have just happened out of thin air."

"What do you mean?"

"I believe someone had knowledge of what was about to happen."

"You think I did?"

"I want to know what you know. For example, did you know that they were capable of carrying out such an atrocity? Did you imagine in your wildest dreams they could do this?"

"Yeah, I fucking knew it."

Reznick was taken aback by O'Keefe's ready admittance.

"Sure, I knew. I knew what kind of guys they were becoming. And that's why I got the hell out. I knew it would come to this. No one listened to me. Not a soul. I talked about it. I told people."

Reznick held up his hand. "Hang on, hang on. You told people?"

O'Keefe shrugged. "That's right. I warned them. But no one listened. I know what my brothers are like. I know them better than anyone. They're bad seeds."

Reznick nodded. "I'll come back to that in a minute. But first, Robert, I'm going to level with you. I'm not going to sugarcoat it. I'm going to be honest with you. Completely honest and transparent. But in return, I would hope you will do the same with me."

O'Keefe nodded. "I have nothing to hide."

"First, what that Fed said? Special Agent Farrelly? That's not true. I'm not a special agent in the traditional sense. But I do report to one of the most senior executives at the FBI on matters pertaining to national security. Do you understand?"

"I think so, yeah. National security. Do you mean classified stuff?"

"Exactly." Reznick rested his hands on his knees, staring straight at O'Keefe. "You've built an enviable life for you and your family. I admire that. It couldn't have been easy."

O'Keefe stared off into the distance. "You have no idea."

"I was lucky . . . I had a father who was around. Who taught me the difference between right and wrong. But from what I understand, you and your brothers weren't so lucky."

"Let me tell you, it was a living nightmare. I hear people talking about how guys like me are privileged. Privileged? They don't know what the fuck they're talking about. I had to work my tail off. People talk about not having much money. Trust me, they don't know what it's like being as poor as we were."

"I understand."

"That was just one part of my fun childhood. You want to talk about the emotional, terrifying impact of a guy like Charlie Campbell on our family?"

Reznick nodded.

"It was hell. From the day he arrived, I knew it would end in bloodshed. I could see the way my brothers looked at Campbell. From the very first day, they worshipped him. But I could see what he was. He was a maniac. Manipulative. He manipulated my mother. And then my brothers. I got out of there as fast as I could."

Reznick appreciated his honesty. But he needed Robert to open up more, so it was time to return the honesty. "It sounds like you've watched some of the coverage on TV about the sniper attacks."

O'Keefe nodded. "It's like a nightmare."

"It was bad. Real bad. As I said, I was there when it happened, with my daughter, when your brothers began firing."

"Is she OK? Your daughter."

"I haven't been able to get in touch with her, but I'm hoping she got to a safe place. Robert, you'll probably find out at some point, but I think it's only right that you know how they died."

"The police? I know how they died."

"No, I mean your brothers."

O'Keefe sipped his drink. "I don't know if I need to know that."

"I think you do." Reznick took a few moments to gather his thoughts. "A guy outside Yankee stadium stopped a motorcyclist at gunpoint, hauled him off the bike, and went after your brothers when they tried to escape."

"The cops mentioned that. That's unbelievable."

Reznick sighed. "I know the full story. Better than anyone. Robert, I was that guy. The guy that went after them."

"I don't understand."

"I was the guy on the motorcycle. I killed them both. I killed your brothers. I wanted you to know that before we go further."

O'Keefe's eyes began to fill with tears.

"I pursued them, and I killed them. I'm not proud of that. But it had to be done."

"I feel sick."

"I'm sorry, for what it's worth. I'm sorry it was me. But it would have been someone else. If I hadn't, they might have killed more cops, or other innocent people, as they made their escape."

O'Keefe wiped the tears from his eyes. "They were bad. But they were my brothers. I hated them. But they were still my blood."

Reznick sighed and stared out over the waves crashing onto the beach in the distance. "I know. The cold, hard fact is that they killed eight cops and wounded quite a few others. That was their doing."

"I don't know what to say."

"Say whatever you want."

O'Keefe's lower lip was quivering.

"It says a lot about you, your character, that you didn't follow that same path," Reznick added. "It must've been hard for you seeing your brothers choose that life."

O'Keefe shook his head. "I wish . . . I wish I could turn the clock back."

Reznick stayed silent.

O'Keefe dabbed his eyes with the back of his hand. "I knew it would end like this. I just knew it. But I never imagined it would be so terrible."

Reznick nodded. "You say you knew it would end like this. What exactly do you mean? Take me back to the beginning."

"It all leads back to Charlie Campbell, my stepfather. That's how it all started. The first day Charlie Campbell came into our lives. He was a racist. A psychopath. And I was scared shitless just being in his presence. He gave off those vibes."

"I read some of Campbell's FBI file on my way over here. But I'd like to hear more about him from you."

"Why? He's dead."

"That's why. I believe his death about three months ago might have been the spark that led your brothers to stage the attack today."

O'Keefe began to break down and shake his head.

Ten

Camila Perez sat down in a booth at her local diner in Hempstead, Long Island, overlooking the parking lot. Her eyes were drawn to the TV behind the counter showing the distressing scenes coming in from Yankee Stadium.

A waitress stopped by and poured her a coffee. "Isn't that terrible?" she said. "Is nothing sacred? It should be a lovely day for people. Police just doing their job. Awful."

Camila shook her head. "I don't understand. So they only killed cops?"

"Chopper blown out of the sky, four civilians killed. But mostly NYPD. My brother-in-law works in the Bronx. He's a cop. Thankfully he wasn't on duty today. But I was just talking to my sister, and she's traumatized, as you can imagine."

"I'm glad your brother-in-law is safe."

"So am I. He's a good man. Anyway, life goes on, right? What can I get you?"

Perez didn't feel like eating, but she needed something to make her feel better. She ordered pancakes with maple syrup. Once she'd finished, and had another cup of coffee, she was feeling marginally better.

She sat alone for the next hour, drinking coffee, scrolling through messages from friends talking about the horrific scenes in the Bronx.

She checked out what people were saying on Twitter about it, but too many people were sharing disturbing blood-soaked cell phone footage taken at the scene. Eventually, she put her phone away.

Perez's thoughts turned to Leon. She wondered when he would call. He had promised to call half an hour earlier because he knew how worried she was. But still nothing.

He worked in downtown Manhattan, miles from the Bronx. But she wondered if the shootings outside Yankee Stadium meant he would have to work later, or would even have trouble leaving Manhattan. She had heard on the radio that subway lines across the Bronx and Manhattan had been shut down for an hour as the police responded to social media rumors that the culprits had been spotted on a subway train.

Her gaze wandered back around the diner. Everyone's attention was seemingly glued to the TV.

She turned and glanced out the window and across the parking lot. Twenty yards away, two young men were sitting in a pickup truck, smoking cigarettes, staring straight at her. Her stomach immediately tightened. They were definitely staring at her. She was the only diner sitting by the window.

The men looked Hispanic, like her. Not unusual in Hempstead. But what set them apart were the gang tattoos on their necks, the distinctive blue-and-white clothes, and the arm out the window sporting numerous gang symbol tattoos which she was very familiar with. MS-13.

Were these the same guys who had threatened Leon? Were they here to threaten her now? And why hadn't Leon called? She felt a growing sense of dread.

Perez turned away from the window, trying not to think about the men—maybe they were there for reasons that had nothing to do with her; maybe she'd only caught their attention because she was near the window. On the TV behind the counter, the terrible images of fleeing crowds outside Yankee Stadium were being shown for the umpteenth time.

She couldn't shake the feeling of grave unease she got from the gangbangers outside. Maybe she should call Leon. Should she call the cops? She imagined they already had too much on their plates to worry about a young woman being stared at through a diner window in broad daylight. The men in the truck weren't doing anything illegal, after all.

Her cell phone rang and she nearly jumped out of her skin. *Leon.*

But she didn't recognize the number on the caller ID. "Yeah, Camila speaking."

She heard only silence, although she sensed someone was there.

"Yeah, who's this?"

"Hey, *Camila speaking*," said a man's voice with a distinctive Salvadoran accent. "You look nice today. Real nice."

Perez turned and saw that the passenger in the pickup was grinning like a jackal, cell phone pressed to his ear. Her heart skipped a beat. How had they gotten her number?

She felt alone and desperately scared as she sat in the booth, listening to the man's breathing. Exposed to their malevolence. Their reach. She had prayed long and hard that they would leave Leon alone.

"What exactly do you want?" she said.

"We don't want anything. We're just here to remind you that our friends are very grateful for your fiancé's help in the past, and they won't forget that. Neither will we. And they've asked us to tell you that if you need anything taken care of, they will be only too glad to help."

"I don't want anything taken care of. Do you understand that? I'd like us to get on with our lives. That's all."

"And you will. Trust me, we want nothing more than to allow you to get back to that real nice fiancé of yours. He's an interesting guy. Talks well."

Perez felt sick at the mess their life had become. It was all down to Leon's weakness of character and his betrayal of his employer. She knew he wasn't a terrible person. And she had rationalized that his were the actions of a desperate man, being blackmailed and in fear for his life. At the mercy of highly dangerous people.

She just wanted it all to end. She wished she had someone she could talk to, other than her priest. But she didn't have anyone. No one to look out for her. And these men probably knew that.

The more she thought about what Leon had done—falsifying reports and passing on classified information to gangsters—the more it hurt. He should have taken a different path. But she also knew that if he had, he would have been killed. Or she would have been. What sort of choice was that? They had him. And there would be no escape.

Somehow Leon would have to live with what he'd done. It seemed like a small price to pay. But there was a bigger price she was paying. An emptiness in her soul that couldn't be repaired.

Perez drank her Coke, not able to look out the window at the men. Her parents would be mortified if they knew what her fiancé was involved in. She had been brought up by her parents—incredibly hardworking people from Mexico—to study hard at school, obey the law, and love everything America had to offer. They had told her since she was a child that she was lucky. That she should cherish the freedoms and the economic opportunities that America offered.

She had obeyed the law her entire life, despite the prevalence of gangs in the neighborhood where she grew up. But Leon had dragged her into his world. His actions and her silence would ultimately define them both on Judgment Day. She would have to atone for her sins in another life. She knew that.

"You still there?" the voice said.

She cleared her throat, pressing the cell phone to her ear. "I don't want to see you again."

"And you won't, we promise. We think it's important that you understand that there can be consequences for making bad decisions." *Bad decisions.* So that was it? They were issuing a not-so-subtle warning for her and Leon not to make bad decisions. Which meant, in her eyes, going to the cops or the Feds. It sent a chill down her spine. "We just want to let you know that we're here, in Hempstead. You know who we are, and we know who you are, and we're cool with that. Don't be afraid of us."

"Afraid of you? But I am. Don't you see that?"

"Listen, miss, no need to be afraid of us. People you need to be afraid of are those crazies shooting up cops outside Yankee Stadium. Now that's fucked up. And in broad daylight."

Perez turned and stared through the diner window at the passenger in the pickup. "Please don't follow me. You need to leave us alone."

"Just so long as you know we have your back."

Eleven

The waters off Southampton were sparkling in the late-afternoon sun. Reznick walked along the beach with the traumatized hedge fund manager. Robert O'Keefe was still struggling to come to terms with the horror his brothers had wreaked. The waves were hitting the sand hard, edging higher up the golden dunes. The soothing sound reminded Reznick of home, sitting by the tiny cove beside his house in Rockland, Maine.

They walked in silence for another hundred yards before Reznick spoke.

"Talk to me about Charlie Campbell. I can read files and prison reports for hours, but I want to know what this guy was really like. Tell me about him. Who was he?"

O'Keefe looked up at the blue sky as if for guidance. "He moved in with my mom a few months after my dad died. My brothers were a lot younger. More impressionable. I was a teenager. I couldn't stand the sight of him."

Reznick was glad that O'Keefe was at least talking. "What exactly was the problem with him?"

"Well, for starters, he had served serious time. In Leavenworth. Aryan Brotherhood inner circle. He brought that whole thing into our house. The hatred. The anger. The knives. The guns. And the drugs."

"What else?"

"I hated him. He wasn't my dad. No one could replace my dad. And certainly not some psychopath like Campbell. Once my mom married that animal, she condemned all of us to a bad future. It began when she started writing to him in prison. No idea why she did it. I think she was lonely."

Reznick nodded.

"She was a religious woman. She believed in God. She believed in the church. And she believed in redemption. She believed she could make him a better person. I suspect she had a Mother Teresa complex. But, God knows, it wasn't a good move for us."

"It must've been a good move for Campbell."

"Very true. When he got out, he had a ready-made family. Mom loved him. I was powerless to do anything about it. I left home as soon as I could, went to college, got a degree in economics, and never looked back. Got a job in an investment bank. But my brothers, they were left behind. I always wished I could've taken them with me, and maybe it wouldn't have come to this. Charlie Campbell molded them from poor rough boys into the murderous bastards you saw today."

"So Charlie Campbell was Aryan Brotherhood?"

"Not just that. He was high up. Very senior."

"When was the last time you saw him?"

O'Keefe brushed some hair out of his eyes as the wind whipped up the beach. "Charlie? When I left—must be fifteen years ago now, maybe more. He tried to be nice to me. To win me over. But he never did. When he died a few months ago, my brother Todd called me. I thought it was strange, as we've been estranged all this time. I think you might be right that this is what it all comes back to. It triggered them. His death triggered them."

"Todd? He's the youngest?"

"Yeah, followed in Campbell's footsteps. Serious prison time. I just turned my back on them all. Didn't want to deal with it. But Todd blamed the cops for what he described as killing his dad. That's what he called him. His *dad*. I told Todd that Charlie Campbell wasn't our dad. Not then. Not ever."

"Go back to what you said. Todd blamed the cops?"

"Yeah."

"For killing Campbell?"

"Exactly."

Reznick turned and looked back and saw Farrelly standing on the sand near the house. The young Fed was speaking into his cell phone, staring down the beach at them, as if relaying the fact that Reznick was talking alone with O'Keefe. Reznick faced Robert, whose head was tilted up into the sun's rays as though he were trying to warm up his mood. "So, he blamed the cops for killing Campbell. What happened?"

"I believe it was a surveillance operation on Campbell. That's what Todd told me."

"What exactly did he tell you?"

"Just that some undercover cops had Campbell and his crew under surveillance, and then they pounced and arrested him. Campbell put up a struggle. And he was killed, some sort of choke hold."

Reznick wondered why Meyerstein had not shared that information about Campbell and how he had died. "Unfortunately, these things happen from time to time."

"Not in Todd's eyes. He blamed the cops. Not only that—he also told me there was going to be a reprisal from the Brand. I was freaking out."

Reznick was beginning to hear a whole new narrative. He wondered why these facts had been omitted from what he'd been told. "Todd made this threat?"

"Right. He said something along the lines of 'the NYPD are going to know what a reprisal means,' or something."

"What kind of reprisal?"

"Todd wasn't specific. He just said the NYPD were going to pay. Campbell was very senior, at least that's what I heard. And Todd said that the word had gone out. Some 'shot caller' had decided? I wasn't too sure what that meant."

"I think it refers to a top guy inside who calls the shots."

"So the word went out."

"Did he give you the name of the person who made this call?"

"No. Just someone in the Aryan Brotherhood leadership. I guarantee you that my two crazy brothers didn't do this without the Brotherhood at least helping them with logistics and giving the go-ahead."

Reznick nodded. "I agree. I have a very important question. And I'm going to ask you to take your time before you answer. Robert, what did you do after your brother made those threats?"

"Well, first I was scared."

"That's natural, trust me."

"Todd has a way of talking. It sounds very much like Campbell, slow, deliberate. Chilling. So . . . I was concerned."

"What did you do after you heard those threats?"

"I called the FBI."

Reznick took a few moments to absorb this information. "I want to make sure I have this right. The FBI had this information three months ago? Are you sure? I mean positive?"

"One billion percent positive. Remember I told you that I told people about what I knew? Well, that's it."

"Who did you call at the FBI?"

"The FBI field office in New York. I googled the number. And I spoke to a guy."

"You spoke to a guy? FBI in lower Manhattan?"

"Yeah, that's right."

"Who in the FBI did you speak to?"

"Special Agent Cortez, I think."

"Cortez. I saw Cortez a couple of hours ago. So what happened?"

"What happened? I don't know what happened. I never heard back from them."

Reznick rubbed his temples. If what O'Keefe was saying were true, it meant the FBI had advance warning of the attack and had failed to act on it.

He patted O'Keefe on the back. "You did the right thing, Robert."

"Fat lot of good it did."

"I need another favor."

"What kind of favor?"

"Can I see your cell phone?"

"Why? I already showed the FBI."

"I just want to check something."

O'Keefe pulled out his cell phone from his pocket and handed it to Reznick.

"Did you use this phone to call the Feds?"

"Yeah."

"Can I have the passcode?"

O'Keefe gave him the passcode. "Do you have a warrant to do that?"

"No, I don't. You don't have to give me permission to do this. But I'm assuming you have nothing to hide."

"I live a straightforward life."

Reznick smiled. "Glad someone does these days." He keyed in the passcode, unlocking the phone. He scrolled down through the contacts. He also made a mental note of O'Keefe's cell phone number. "Bear with me now." Reznick walked down to the water's edge, pulled out his own cell phone, and called a hacker he knew.

"Hey, Mr. R., how goes it?"

"Not much time, my friend. I've got a cell phone number." Reznick gave him Robert O'Keefe's number. "I want to know if and when this cell phone contacted the FBI field office in New York within the last three months."

"Why do you want to know that, man? Is it connected to what happened at the Yankee game today?"

"Yup."

"Man, that's terrible."

"I know. I was there."

"I saw the footage. It's horrific."

Reznick cleared his throat. "Can you help? I want to check whether the guy who owns this cell phone is telling the truth."

"I'll get back to you ASAP."

Twelve

The twelve-story federal Metropolitan Correctional Center in lower Manhattan was close to the FBI's New York field office. Meyerstein headed down a series of brightly lit corridors flanked by four FBI special agents and a surly prison guard, keys jangling from his belt. Cameras watching her every move, the sound of metal doors clanking behind her. She didn't show it, but she felt uneasy. It was hard not to.

They passed through electronic doors and into the high-security unit, 10 South, which housed only the prisoners deemed the most dangerous, while they awaited trial. The inmate she was going to meet had been charged with murdering a leader of the Black Mafia Family street gang, conspiracy to murder a fellow inmate, and racketeering.

Meyerstein followed the guard until they came to a windowless room with just a desk and two chairs chained to the concrete floor.

The guard smirked. "Make yourself at home. He'll be with you in a little while. Don't try and provoke him. Guy is ready to blow at any minute."

Meyerstein forced a smile. "Appreciate the advice." She went inside with the two special agents by her side; the other two agents waited outside. She stood, hands clasped in front of her.

Meyerstein was surprised the inmate had agreed to see her. He had a reputation for extreme violence—stabbings and hits. She had read his file. The man had connections she was hoping he could leverage. But whether he would listen to her proposition was another matter.

Meyerstein sighed and began to flick through messages on her cell phone. Another from O'Donoghue requesting a preliminary report and another from the FBI's senior legal counsel wanting to discuss the *Jon Reznick issue*. She could see O'Donoghue was seriously concerned how it would look if Reznick's involvement in the FBI, stretching back several years, were revealed.

She wondered if O'Donoghue was going to use Reznick's very public pursuit of the snipers as an opportunity to end the Bureau's relationship with him. Was it possible that O'Donoghue would really try to cut all ties to Jon Reznick on the same day that Reznick had hunted down the two snipers and taken them out? It was perverse. She viewed it as treachery, nothing more, nothing less. Political expediency. But increasingly she had felt at odds with her senior colleagues, all highly experienced intelligence experts, who questioned the wisdom of having a former black-ops assassin working for the FBI on classified investigations.

Meyerstein understood their concerns. She might have had the same misgivings herself if she were in their place. But she knew too well not only what Reznick was capable of but how his skill set had augmented the FBI's at critical moments. A couple years earlier, he'd even managed to rescue her after the Russian Mafia had kidnapped her. Reznick, not her senior colleagues, had come through for her. She considered him invaluable both for the dangerous work he did for her and across the FBI and for his ability to act as her sounding board, as and when required.

The clanging of electronic doors slamming shut snapped Meyerstein out of her musings.

A huge, fearsome-looking white man, heavily tattooed—swastikas on his forearms—was standing in the doorway, flanked by two hulking prison officers.

The prisoner shuffled into the room wearing shower slides. He was classic Aryan Brotherhood: Celtic crosses on his neck, ice-blue eyes staring at her.

Thomas "Mad Dog" Mills was handcuffed with chains on his legs. He had arms like lamb shanks. The officer pointed his nightstick at a chair behind the desk.

Mills shuffled over, sat down, and grimaced. His malevolent gaze wandered around the room for a few moments.

Meyerstein waited. Eventually, Mills fixed his gaze on her for what seemed like an eternity, as if trying to unnerve her. Then he again looked around the room at the special agents, staring at them long and hard, before smiling. The guy seemed to be enjoying the attention Meyerstein's visit had brought.

"This is a real treat," Mills drawled. "They don't allow anyone to see me. Not a goddamn soul. I'm guessing you must be someone pretty special."

Meyerstein said nothing, content to let him do the talking for a bit. Get it out of his system.

"They didn't say who you were or what you wanted."

Meyerstein just stared back at him. She wasn't going to let him intimidate her.

"Who are you?" he asked.

"My name is Martha Meyerstein. I'm an assistant director at the FBI."

"Is that right?"

Meyerstein nodded.

"FBI, huh? Now why would I want to talk to you? I don't like people like you. Don't you understand that? Read my fucking file. I loathe the Feds. I loathe the government. All types of government."

"I'm not really interested in whether you like people like me or not, Thomas. If you like the government or don't like the government. That's your prerogative."

"Why are you here?"

"I'm here to talk. And just so you know, I don't give a damn about your reputation."

Mills sat and stared, expression impassive.

"I'm going to be blunt, Thomas. I'm here to make a deal. Just me and you. No one else will be privy to it."

Mills looked over again at the two young Feds at the other side of the room. "These your friends?"

"They're FBI special agents."

Mills fixed his gaze on them like a wolf eyeing its prey. "Well, good for them. Real nice dressers. Got to let me know where you guys get your suits. Very sharp. I know a guy from Hong Kong who visits Chinatown to measure up some of the Triad dudes. Helluva nice fella."

"Enough of the wisecracks." Meyerstein leaned forward. "This is how it's going to work."

Mills turned his attention back to her. His face was flushed, veins bulging in his neck. "Meyerstein, huh? How do you spell that? I'm guessing M-e-y-e-r-s-t-e-i-n," he said, picking out each letter of her surname. "I don't know many Meyersteins. In fact, I don't know any, to be honest. Not where I'm from. Is that an American name?"

"Born and bred."

"Where's your family from?"

"Midwest."

"Where in the Midwest?"

"Chicago."

"Got a lot of associates up in Chicago. Real tight crew up there."

Meyerstein sighed.

Mills sniffed and cleared his throat. "It's a tough town, I'll give you that."

"It has its moments."

"Know what they call this part of the prison?"

Meyerstein nodded.

"First time in 10 South?"

She knew he was verbally sparring with her to show he had the upper hand. She had to be patient and put up with it. But she could already sense his deep rage and animosity, which was not far from the surface. "Yes, it is."

"You liking it?"

"Seen worse."

"It's a real fucking shithole. This is the place they held El Chapo. John Gotti. All the big names if they're on trial in the city."

"So I've heard."

Mills shifted in his seat and grimaced. "I've written a letter to my attorney." He leaned forward. She could smell the coffee and tobacco on his breath. "You know why?"

"You don't like it here, right?"

Mills grinned, enjoying her discomfort at being so close to him. "You know, people always seem on edge when I'm around. I can look into your eyes and tell exactly what you feel about me. I sense fear. Animalistic trait in me, I guess."

He sat back. His pupils were like pinpricks. "This place is designed to make people go insane. The fluorescent lights are always on. There's never any quiet. Do you know what I'm saying?"

"I'm not here to talk about your living conditions, Thomas. At least not directly."

"So, what the hell *are* you here for?"

"What if I said I might be able to get you out of here?"

Mills shrugged his huge shoulders, chains rattling on the floor.

"You see, I'm in a position to put in a word for you. Actually, it's more than a word. I can get you out of here. I can get you transferred to any jail where you might feel more at home. Any jail."

"Is that right?"

"I can put in calls. I can pull strings. We're reasonable people."

Mills's gaze wandered around the windowless room. He stared at the impassive expressions of the two FBI special agents. "Reasonable people, huh? What do you guys think? Are you two reasonable people?"

The special agents just stared back at him.

Meyerstein said, "I hear you're in your cell twenty-three hours a day. Can't be much fun."

Mills looked at her, eyes cold and dead. "Sometimes twenty-four. Depends on the mood of the guards." His gaze pierced hers. "Tell me, where do you live?"

Meyerstein shifted in her seat. "Why do you want to know that?"

"Just curious, I guess."

"This isn't about me. This is about you, Thomas. I want to do something to help you."

Mills arched his eyebrows. "Help me? Now why's a nice Jewish FBI agent offering to do a guy like me a favor?"

"You're a shot caller on the East Coast. Maybe *the* shot caller. We have reason to believe that a letter you recently sent to your sister, which we became aware of only a few hours ago, contained coded instructions that a hit was to be carried out."

Mills said nothing.

Meyerstein pulled a photocopy of the letter from her jacket. "Here's the thing. We visited her house. And she still had it lying around. Written in invisible ink, perhaps your urine, were instructions. Very clever. You confess everything now, I can get you moved to a better prison, a far better prison, maybe back to Florence, Colorado. You were there before Leavenworth, weren't you?"

Mills grinned. "I love the fresh air of Colorado. I like the people there."

"You'll be with the rest of your crew. Better food. Protection. The works. And that's not all. We can slash your sentence . . . We can make recommendations, confidentially, that you get four years in Florence, not forty. We can do that. And this could really turn things around for you. Now you really need to think about this. Four years. No one else is ever going to get an offer like that. But we are prepared to do this."

"That's all very interesting. And what is it that I'm supposed to confess to you?"

"I'm getting to that. I'm guessing, Thomas, that you heard about what happened at Yankee Stadium this morning."

"A guard mentioned it. You want to tell me about it?"

Meyerstein smiled. He was playing dumb. But he wasn't dumb. She had read a psychologist's report that said he had an IQ of 143. She knew he was very well read. He frequently quoted the German philosopher Goethe. "Earlier today, as you know, two of the O'Keefe brothers, aligned with the Aryan Circle, a splinter group of the Aryan Brotherhood of Texas, killed eight police officers outside Yankee Stadium."

Mills cleared his throat. "You're saying they killed eight officers? Damn, that's pretty hard-core."

"It was cold-blooded murder, that's what it was. Nothing hard-core about killing police officers. And we believe you were the shot caller on this. You and three of the O'Keefe brothers were all in Leavenworth at the same time. We've seen the coded letter to your sister. We're checking the phone records from here." Meyerstein smiled. "We'll be checking the guards' cell phones too, in case you were wondering. We believe, in this instance, that someone within the Brotherhood is calling the shots. Maybe it's you. I don't know. Maybe someone in Florence. But someone is pulling the strings on this operation."

"Go on."

"We know Todd O'Keefe is a lieutenant of yours, that he was an enforcer inside Leavenworth. On the outside, like a lot of your guys, he carries out hits. But only when you or someone of your seniority gives it the green light. You see, I'm not convinced this is over. A few of my colleagues also believe there might be another attack. Imminently."

73

"That's an interesting story, Meyerstein. I'm sitting here really blown away by this whole imagination of yours. It must've taken the FBI all of five minutes to come up with that implausible scenario. Very creative."

Meyerstein sighed and shifted in her seat. She felt soiled just sitting so close to such a monster. She had read about how he had stabbed his rivals in the Brotherhood. Beat several black inmates to death. Shanked a black guard. Took out the eye of another. But with no bead on Todd O'Keefe's location, she needed to make a deal if they stood a chance of stopping any further attacks. "Interestingly, it wasn't Todd who killed those officers this morning. So did he delegate it to his brothers, or was that your idea?"

Mills shrugged.

"They're both dead, in case you were wondering."

"I don't know anything about this. Especially since I'm in solitary."

"They were killed before they got out of the Bronx."

"Listen, what has that got to do with me? You think I'm some redneck peckerwood?"

"No, I think you're smart. And you need to listen up, Thomas. The letter sent to your sister has your fingerprints all over it, and your code isn't hard to figure out. We believe that you ordered these killings to avenge Charlie Campbell. And only you can get the message out to stop this."

"I haven't seen Charlie in years."

"But you stayed in touch. And when his stepsons landed in Leavenworth, you took them under your wing."

Mills shrugged, icy eyes locked onto hers.

"We need to find Todd O'Keefe."

"Let me tell you something, Meyer*stein*. Charlie Campbell was a brother to me. A crazy, tough fuck, but a blood brother. Now, you won't see guys like me weeping over Charlie. We know the business we're in and who we roll with. It can get you killed. But we're all prepared to die. Dying is no big thing. You don't seem to realize that."

74

Mills was getting more animated talking about Campbell. Meyerstein could see how close the men had been. "We're offering you the best deal you're ever going to get, Thomas. A deal that will set you free in four years. I've seen people in New York facing Class D violent felonies who served seven years. We're offering four, despite everything we know about you. Think about that. You might scoff at such expediency. But I don't. I want to save innocent people getting killed."

Mills shook his head.

"You're not going to get a better deal than that."

"You think this is a negotiating tactic? Gimme a break. You come in here, thinking I'm going to talk. Thinking you'll do what you can and make it all stop."

"I came in here willing to strike a deal. You can take it, and it can make your life a whole lot easier."

"You don't get it, do you? You just don't fucking get it."

"Get what?"

"Get what makes us tick. What makes us who we are. Do you think the AB are stupid?"

"No, I don't."

"We're many things, but stupid isn't one of them. Don't you think the other guys in the AB will wonder why I'm getting out so early?"

"The prison can say that they're transferring you."

Mills sneered. "Wake the fuck up. They won't buy that bullshit. We have people everywhere. And I mean everywhere. They'll want to know where I've been for the past twenty minutes, who I've been talking to. I guarantee you word's already gotten out."

"There is a deal. It's on the table. My advice? Take it."

"By informing on a brother? You think that's gonna cut it with me?"

"You're a father. And I'm guessing your children would like to be closer to you."

"My children hate me. Disowned me. So did my parents, years ago. My first wife killed herself. But I'm sure you already know all that."

"Make the deal, and we can make sure no more innocent blood is spilled."

"See . . . that's where you're wrong. You've put your cards on the table. Well, I'm going to put mine on the table, Meyerstein. From what I read, the cops weren't innocent. It was a choke hold, five of them on top of Charlie, and his heart couldn't take it. And sometimes . . . you've got to send a message. Because if you don't, it'll happen again. And again. They need to know we look after our own. And we take care of business how we see fit."

"Killing people is not taking care of business."

Mills stretched his neck muscles. "That's where you're wrong. Understand this: if the brothers this morning hadn't been taken out, you would have been facing massacres in multiple locations. So don't think this is over. In fact, I wouldn't be surprised if someone is going to wreak whatever havoc they can."

"No more blood needs to be shed."

Mills sighed. "It's the only language people understand. Violence, blood, death."

"Is that your final word? I'm reaching out to you, Thomas, face-to-face, and it's the last chance you'll get of ever being a free man."

Mills smiled. "I was never a free man. That's a fucking illusion. No one is free. We're all in chains. I'm in chains. You're in chains. My advice to you, Meyerstein? Get the body bags ready. This ain't over. Not till we say so."

Thirteen

Reznick was standing alone on the beach in Southampton after Robert O'Keefe headed back into his house to take an urgent call from his boss. He was about to make a call of his own when his cell phone rang.

"Hi, Dad," Lauren said.

Reznick sagged with relief to hear her voice. "Thank God."

"I'm sorry, I tried to call, but there are cell phone signal problems across the city, apparently."

Reznick closed his eyes for a moment. He wanted to hug her tight. "Lauren, listen to me. Are you OK?"

"I'm OK, Dad. You can relax."

"Where are you? Are you back at the hotel or your apartment?"

"I made it back to the hotel, eventually. It was a nightmare. The cab driver dropped us all off."

"Are you still there?"

"No, I'm not, I—"

"Why not?"

"Dad, I'm not hiding away like some frightened rabbit. I don't scare easily."

"Where are you now?"

"I'm in an Uber, headed to Midtown to see some friends. I just heard a rumor on Facebook that they might cancel the fireworks. It's the Fourth of July! Where's that famous New York City grit? We're not going to be intimidated. I for one don't want to cower in my apartment or hotel room."

Reznick closed his eyes again. "Midtown? You need to listen to me."

"Dad—"

"Lauren, you need to listen up. This is not over. What happened this morning, it could happen again. You need to get back to your apartment or the hotel and stay there until I give the all clear. Buy whatever food or drinks you want, and put it on my room. Take your friends there too. But you need to get off the streets."

"Forget it."

"The attacks are not over. The snipers this morning? There might be more of them."

"There might not. I can't live like that, Dad. Who do you think I am?"

"Do you understand how serious this is?"

"Of course I do. I just think that you tend to go a little nuts on me, being super protective."

If the situation were less dangerous, he would have smiled at how headstrong she was. Just like her mother. Losing Elisabeth on 9/11 had ripped his heart out by its roots. A part of him died that day. A part of his soul was destroyed. But he knew one thing for sure, that if something happened to Lauren, it would be too much for him to endure. He couldn't take that. He could take a lot. But that would crush him. Kill him.

"It's my job to protect you, Lauren."

"Listen, this morning was terrible. But we can't just hide. That's what these nutcases want us to do."

"Don't you understand? I'm not asking you to hide. I'm asking you to listen to me and use some common sense. Besides, these nutcases aren't looking to spread fear. They just want to kill. So far it's just cops. But that might change."

"I was there. I get it. We were under attack."

"I asked you to head back to the hotel or your apartment and stay there. Now you're telling me you're in a goddamn Uber headed to Midtown. That's ridiculous. Get safe, get inside. Not hanging out in a public space."

"I can't live like that, and besides, you're not here. You're not safe, are you? I'm assuming you're part of a team involved in tracking these people down."

"I'm telling you, Lauren, you do as you're told, do you hear me?" Reznick kicked away a small rock that had washed up on the beach. "Do not go out in public places until we have the all clear. We'll talk when this is over, but for now, get inside. And remember one thing: I love you."

"Love you too, Dad. But I'm not going to hide away. New Yorkers stand together at times like these. Besides, if those bastards think they can scare us, then they can think again. To hell with them. This is America. It's the Fourth of July, after all."

Reznick ended the call and stared out over the water. He couldn't believe how headstrong she was, though he shouldn't be surprised after the events of last summer. He wondered whether he should text her to call him when she eventually made it back to the hotel. But he figured that would just rile her up further.

He turned and started up the beach toward Robert O'Keefe's oceanfront home when his cell phone rang again.

"Mr. R., OK to talk?" The Miami hacker.

Reznick was pleased to hear his voice. "Sure, go ahead."

"So, the guy, Robert Joseph O'Keefe, did contact the Feds directly. Was transferred to an extension belonging to Leon Cortez. Three minutes and thirty-one seconds the call lasted."

Reznick took a few moments to process the information. This meant that the FBI were aware, or should have been made aware, *three months ago*, about the threat posed by the O'Keefe brothers. But why hadn't measures been taken to haul in the O'Keefes? Also, why hadn't Meyerstein mentioned this? It didn't seem credible that Cortez wouldn't have passed the tip higher up the chain within the FBI. Or maybe he had, but the information had gotten lost or the threat level downgraded after an initial investigation.

The problem with intel was that it was jealously guarded. Sometimes not shared among other intelligence agencies as much as it should be. Sometimes not even *within* a single intelligence agency. Was it possible that the field office in New York hadn't alerted the higher ranks of the FBI? Reznick knew from bitter experience that even good intel sometimes got lost among a deluge of shit intel. And sometimes just simple sloppiness.

"Something else," the hacker said.

"I'm listening."

"The NYPD left a message, a couple of months back, asking Robert O'Keefe to return their call."

"So the NYPD were aware too. Interesting. And?"

"The message was from a cop named Jimmy Greer. He gave a direct gang unit number for NYPD at their HQ in lower Manhattan and a cell phone number."

"Can you text me this guy's name and cell phone number and the NYPD number?"

"Gimme a second . . ."

A ping emanated from Reznick's phone.

"Done."

"Got it. Really appreciate that. One more thing. This is time critical. Tell me this guy's location, at this moment."

"According to his cell phone, Jimmy Greer is hanging out at . . . a place called the Corner Bar in Sag Harbor, Long Island."

Reznick ran the idea around his head. Sag Harbor was only a twenty-minute drive away.

"Hey, Mr. R.? Good luck. And if you need me, whatever the hell you're doing, I'll be right here."

"I know you will. I really appreciate it."

"You got it."

Reznick was trying to piece together how the cop, Jimmy Greer, fit into the whole thing. Maybe the FBI's New York field office had brought their concerns to the NYPD? He walked back up the beach to the house. Farrelly was having coffee at the kitchen table and talking to O'Keefe. "Robert, I appreciate your time in such difficult circumstances," Reznick said. "You mind if I have a quick couple of minutes before I head off?"

O'Keefe got up from his seat, and they headed through to a sun-filled study on the other side of the house. Floor-to-ceiling windows overlooked the beach. "What's on your mind?"

"A few things, actually. You said you spoke with someone at the FBI about your concerns?"

"That's correct. I told them what Todd said when he called me. I was concerned."

"You did the right thing. What about the NYPD? Have they ever been in contact with you?"

"A couple of hours ago."

"No, I mean, maybe in the last few months."

O'Keefe frowned. "Oh yeah, I remember, I also contacted the NYPD after Todd's call. I gave a dispatch officer the information, then I got a voice mail that said to give an officer in the gang unit, Jimmy something, a call."

"What did Jimmy say?"

"I left him a message with the same information. That time, I got a call back on my home number from the Department of Justice."

"What?"

"They said they'd made note of my concerns and were investigating. And that was that."

Reznick's senses switched on at hearing that the DOJ had been involved. He could see there was a lot more to that morning's sniper attack than met the eye. It seemed like the O'Keefes had been on the radar of multiple agencies for months. Which begged the obvious question: Why hadn't they been detained and questioned, at the very least? "Let me just make sure I have this all straight. So you alerted the authorities, both NYPD and FBI?"

"Absolutely. Why wouldn't I?"

"Robert, I'm worried about your brother Todd."

"You should be. He's crazy. I mean, very, very dangerous. He's always been nice to me—don't get me wrong. But I know what he's like. What he's capable of. He killed a neighbor's cat when he was ten."

"Shit. Listen, I'm guessing whatever he's feeling, whatever desire he has to avenge your stepfather, will only be exacerbated by your brothers' deaths. I'm concerned that Todd is planning to kill again."

O'Keefe nodded. "He'll want payback. Trust me, you need to find him. Todd is definitely the most dangerous one of the family."

Fourteen

The car headed through the toll plaza and into the Holland Tunnel on the way to lower Manhattan.

Todd O'Keefe was sitting in the back of the SUV being driven by the bartender from the clubhouse. He knew there were license plate readers across the city, and they'd be looking for a car connected to him. But changing vehicles and using cabs was a way around that.

He began to do some breathing exercises. He had rehearsed in his mind over and over again what was going to happen. He had even scoped out the locations. The groundwork had been laid. He had a picture, in his mind's eye, of what he was going to do.

The tunnel lights flashed by. Closer and closer. He had been dreaming of this day for weeks.

O'Keefe felt wired, grinding his teeth. He had popped some amphetamine pills and had snorted a few lines of coke. He was feeling top-line crazy. Just the way he liked. The lights whizzed by.

"You want to talk about the minivan?" the driver asked.

"Let's hear it."

"It's on the level you want. It's already in position. Inside is everything you need."

"When was it dropped off?"

"Just over an hour ago by an associate of ours."

O'Keefe sniffed hard as his mind flashed back to his previous visit. The parking garage gave him the perfect line of sight for what he planned to do next.

"I'm sorry about your brothers, man."

O'Keefe said nothing. He just stared ahead at the tunnel, the headlights of oncoming vehicles making him squint his eyes occasionally. For a second, he was back in the woods near his childhood home in upstate New York. Exploring with Travis and Ryan, each of them with a flashlight. Sometimes they'd camp out there in the summer. And build fires. They sat around talking. As the youngest, he just listened. They talked of robbing, stealing, to get money for their mother. She was broke. And so it had begun: they stole anything they could get their hands on. Eggs from barns, tools from houses, laptops and clothes from out-of-towners' vacation homes. They took it all.

O'Keefe closed his eyes for a few moments, lost in memory. He remembered when their oldest brother, Robert—Bobby—found out. Bobby had looked at the three of them as if they were dirt. Todd couldn't understand it. They had brought in money for their mother, and food. They had the best organic eggs in upstate New York ever since they had stolen some hens and kept them in their garden. It was shortly after that that the police became regular visitors to the house. The cops hauled Todd, Ryan, and Travis out of the family home while their mother screamed, trying to hang on to them. The cops just sneered. Called them poor white trash. He knew they were poor. He also knew they were white. But they were never trash. They wanted to survive. They weren't going to live on handouts.

Then Charlie Campbell came into their lives.

Charlie became their dad. He took the brothers under his wing. He showed them how to catch rabbits. Hares. Deer. Skin them. Gut them. Cook them. Eat them. And he taught them to fight. They fought like crazies. He demanded they fight. Always fight. When the kids who lived nearby mocked them for not having cool clothes, they got their lights knocked out. And so the police came back. The ritual was repeated again, again, and again.

"Maybe I shouldn't have said anything about that," the driver said, snapping O'Keefe from his reverie. "I mean, God rest their souls."

O'Keefe nodded. "My brothers were tough. And they understood that sometimes you've got to sacrifice yourself. For the greater good. For the cause. For what we believe in."

The driver nodded.

"How long you been out?"

"Five years."

"How you finding it?"

"Tough. Family. Money. Cops. The usual shit."

O'Keefe nodded. "I might not make it out of Manhattan after tonight. You have to know that."

"Find a way. We'll help you disappear for good. For years if need be. I know a ton of people that'll help you. But for today, you need anything, you know where the clubhouse is. The shot caller got your number?"

"Yeah, we're all set."

They exited the tunnel, and the skyscrapers of lower Manhattan loomed large. Traffic was clogged up for a block or two because of construction. Eventually, the car pulled up at a red light.

O'Keefe looked at the people strolling on sidewalks, talking into their cell phones, eating hot dogs while walking their dogs. A black guy wearing a smart gray suit on the crosswalk, checking messages on his cell phone. Cell phones had been widespread when he was put away. But it seemed to O'Keefe, since he'd been out, that everyone was using them all the time now. Streaming music, sending messages, emails, surfing the net, Snapchat.

The lights changed and the SUV pulled away. They drove on in silence for a few more blocks until they reached Greenwich Street.

O'Keefe felt his heart beginning to beat a little faster as they drove up to the sixth level of the parking garage. The driver reversed into a space and switched off the engine. He scanned the deserted garage. Then he turned and pointed to a minivan parked at the far end of the lot. "That's it." He rifled in his pockets and handed the keys to O'Keefe. "The bag, everything you need, it's already in there."

O'Keefe took a moment. "The cops always laughed at us. Said we were poor white trash."

The driver nodded.

"We're going to send the cops a final message tonight. They sent Charlie home in a body bag. Well, guess what, same is going to happen to their guys tonight."

The driver hugged O'Keefe tight. "Blood in, blood out, brother."

O'Keefe got out of the SUV and watched the driver pull away. He was on his own now. The way he liked it. He headed over to the van, which was parked with its back to the wall. It had tinted windows as he had requested. He pressed the fob, opening the driver's door, and slid into the front seat. The bag was at his feet.

He reached over and opened the glove compartment. Inside were the military-grade binoculars.

O'Keefe picked up the bag and binoculars and climbed into the back of the van. He leaned forward and opened the back window. His position was perfectly concealed from the street by a low concrete wall topped with metal bars above. He trained the binoculars on the busy downtown street. The coffee shop was located on Trinity Place, perhaps 100 yards away, 120 at a push.

He scanned the sidewalk as pedestrians strolled by the café, oblivious to what was about to happen. A few were standing outside chatting, coffees in hand; a workman wearing a hard hat was talking into his phone.

O'Keefe felt the sweat on his forehead, wiping it away with the back of his shirtsleeve.

He unzipped the bag and pulled out a rifle case, opened it up. Sniper rifle. He mounted the scope. He checked that it was securely mounted to the base. He aimed through the metal bars. Then he began to focus the reticle on the scope. The pedestrians on the street were blurred. A few adjustments. Suddenly, pin-sharp focus through the crosshairs.

He listened to his breathing as he stared into the scope. He felt his anger begin to rise. A black anger, putrid hate, at people he didn't know. People unaware of who he was. And why he was there. They would never understand. Never comprehend the choices he made. He thought again of Travis and Ryan. He assumed it was cops who had killed them too.

His stomach tightened. They'd been prepared to lay down their lives. Prepared to die. Prepared to fight, no matter what or why. They'd carried out orders. Like good soldiers. *Blood in, blood out.* And all for Charlie Campbell, the man who had taken them under his wing. A man who had taught them to shoot. To hunt. To fight. And to kill. They saw, like he did, the way Campbell had looked lovingly at their mother. Protective. Their biological father had left them. Abandoned them. But Campbell stayed by their side until they were old enough to look after themselves. Charlie Campbell taught them everything he knew.

The more he thought of Campbell, the more he felt a primeval rage within him.

Campbell was a cold-blooded killer, the authorities said. But O'Keefe knew the type of man Campbell really was. He was cut from that same cloth. *Blood in, blood out.* He remembered listening as a boy while Campbell spoke of being prepared to kill. To defend your race. To defend your blood.

O'Keefe was staring through the crosshairs and wondered how long he would have to wait. It might be a while. But he knew that in New

York City, and especially in Manhattan, and most especially around lower Manhattan, there were cops everywhere.

And sure enough, a few minutes later, a cop car pulled up outside the coffee shop. Two female cops got out. One headed into the shop while the other leaned against her cruiser, talking into her cell phone.

O'Keefe felt his heart racing as if he'd taken a shot of speed. He lined up the crosshairs, perfectly focused on the cop outside. He held his breath. Savoring the moment. The pleasure of the soon-to-come release. The rush of emotions that would follow. But more than that, the payback for Charlie Campbell. His dad. Blood brother.

O'Keefe controlled his breathing like he'd been taught. He centered the scope. The first cop emerged from the shop laughing, carrying two large coffees. He felt his finger on the trigger. The cop's face was in the center of the crosshairs. Slowly, he squeezed the trigger. A shot rang out. The cop fell, direct hit to the face, blood exploding on the sidewalk and her uniform. The second cop was in his crosshairs, bending over her colleague, radioing for backup. He squeezed twice, hitting her in the back.

The second cop slumped on top of her dead colleague.

Panic as people fled in all directions.

Fuck them.

O'Keefe pulled the van window shut. Put the rifle in the bag. Got back in the front seat. He started up the minivan and quietly pulled away, then headed out of the parking garage and back onto the streets of lower Manhattan.

Charlie Campbell would be avenged.

O'Keefe gave a wry smile as he moved to his next location in the city.

Fifteen

When Reznick's cell phone rang, he was riding up front with the FBI driver on the short journey from Southampton to Sag Harbor.

"Jon, two cops have just been killed in lower Manhattan." Meyerstein's voice sounded strained.

Reznick felt sick as he listened to the details of the cold-blooded attack.

"We just got footage from a parking garage. It's Todd O'Keefe. He's in the city. And he's clearly been given support. Somewhere to lie low. I'd really prefer if you were back in the city right now, Jon. I don't think Todd is going to stop there."

"What about Farrelly?"

"We've instructed him to stay with Robert O'Keefe and his family until we get backup."

"I want to talk to you about something, Martha. After talking to Robert, I think the FBI needs to look at its files again. I have reason to believe that he informed both the FBI and the NYPD that his brother Todd was going to do something. He was very concerned—"

"Do something?" She sounded dubious. "What do you mean by that?"

"Avenge Charlie Campbell, their stepfather."

"I've gone over our file on the O'Keefes. There is no heads-up from Robert O'Keefe on Todd."

"You're wrong."

"Excuse me?"

"Martha, I'm telling you, something is not right. I have proof that Robert O'Keefe is not lying."

"What kind of proof?"

"Not the sort that will hold up in court without a warrant, but that doesn't matter."

"Jon, I don't like your tone of voice. You're insinuating that we didn't act on information that could've prevented this."

"I'm sorry, but it's true. He contacted the FBI. And the cops." Reznick tapped his fingers against the back of the phone and decided to plunge ahead. "I got someone to check Robert O'Keefe's cell phone records. He had a conversation that lasted exactly three minutes and thirty-one seconds with Special Agent Leon Cortez of New York."

"Leon Cortez?"

"Correct. That's all I know. But after that call, Robert O'Keefe never heard back from Cortez or the Feds."

"OK, that is concerning. But there's nothing in the file on this, so I'm assuming that whatever he had to say wasn't important. You'd be surprised how many people report things but are reluctant to give us the details we actually need in order to take their claims seriously."

"Robert O'Keefe has no reason to lie. After he spoke with Cortez, he called the NYPD. Shortly after that, he said he got a call from the Department of Justice, saying that they had taken over the case from the NYPD. Something is seriously wrong here."

Meyerstein was quiet for a minute. "What you're saying is that this was either ignored or buried."

"That's exactly what I'm saying."

Meyerstein groaned. "I'll look into it. You have my word. But it's probably best if you head back. Right now."

"I've come all the way out to the East End of Long Island. We're in Sag Harbor."

"What the hell is in Sag Harbor?"

"The cop Robert O'Keefe was in touch with. Someone that may know more about this whole fuckup."

"Look, I cut you some slack to follow up a lead. But I'm not so sure Sag Harbor is where you need to be right now."

"Maybe. Maybe not. I think Robert O'Keefe is credible. I believe him. And I'd like to hear what this cop has to say."

"You could be on a wild goose chase. The omission from the file might be entirely innocent."

"Maybe. But I'm convinced that at least some people in the FBI and the NYPD knew a hell of a lot more than you and I have been told."

"That is a big, big call, Jon."

"You better believe it. But something doesn't smell right."

"Look, I think your particular . . . skill set . . . might be better deployed back in the city. I'm worried Todd O'Keefe is going to pop up again. And the next time, God knows what he'll do."

"Gimme an hour."

"Not a second more. Then you head back to Manhattan."

"You got it."

The Corner Bar was a run-down saloon in decidedly upscale Sag Harbor. Faded flag decorations hung above the front door, fluttering in the summer breeze. Reznick pulled up a stool at the bar and ordered a beer. It was like an old fisherman's haunt, a few old-timers hanging around. The TV was showing live footage from lower Manhattan, the scene of the attack on the two female cops.

An old man wearing a Mariners cap, sitting on a stool beside him, was shaking his head, nursing a whiskey. "What sort of animals do that?"

Reznick nodded and took a couple of welcome gulps of cold beer.

"Cops? Killing cops? On the Fourth of July? What the hell? Is this America?"

Reznick stared at the TV. The old-timer beside him wouldn't believe what sort of day he'd had. Which was probably just as well. He had been in the thick of it. And then some.

"What the hell is going on in this country?"

A voice behind him said, "Nobody respects cops no more."

Reznick turned around and saw a red-faced, burly guy sitting alone at a table, drinking a pint of beer.

"It's a fucking disgrace," the red-faced guy said. "You hear what I said?"

"I hear you," Reznick said. "You're 100 percent correct."

The guy had tears in his eyes. "Fucking outrageous. Killing cops? Back in the day, that was rare. But now, it's like every fucking second day, I hear about a cop being shot or killed or targeted. On duty outside a ball game? And now two officers gunned down on a coffee break. What the hell is going on?"

The old man with the Mariners cap whispered in Reznick's ear, "Guy used to be in the NYPD. That's why he's so upset."

Reznick nodded. He finished his beer and ordered two more. He picked them up and went over and sat down opposite the red-faced guy. He pushed the bottle toward him. "Here, on me."

The guy stared at the TV screen, shaking his head. "Sorry, I don't know you. What's that for?"

"Take it."

"I'm sorry about getting all emotional over this shit."

"Nothing to apologize for." Reznick reached over to shake the guy's hand. "My name's Jon Reznick."

"Hey, Jon . . ." The guy had a viselike grip. "Jimmy Greer. Unbelievable. Independence Day, and they're killing cops in New York City."

Reznick sipped his beer as his gaze wandered around the bar. He looked at Greer. "It's a bad scene outside Yankee Stadium. I got caught up in the shootings this morning."

"You serious?"

Reznick nodded.

"In the name of Christ. This morning? You OK?"

"I'm fine."

"Where you from?" Greer asked.

"Maine."

"So, you visiting New York. Long way to take in a Yankees game."

"Daughter lives in New York in the summer."

"Maine, huh? Never been there. Supposed to be nice."

"It's like Sag Harbor. On the water. Quiet. Decent."

"You a Yankees fan from Maine?"

"No, just wanted to take my daughter to a game."

"And you and her were there this morning? That's bad fucking luck, man."

Reznick nodded. "We were both there, waiting in line."

"She OK?"

"Yeah, she's back in Manhattan."

"She needs to stay off the streets."

"That's what I told her. Whether she does or not is another matter."

Greer nodded. "Kids never listen. My kids are the same. Fucking law unto themselves."

Reznick went up to the bar and got two more beers, then sat back down beside Greer.

"You don't need to do that," Greer said.

"Forget it." Reznick took a few gulps of the beer and looked up at the TV. He turned to face Greer, lowering his voice. "Jimmy, I was speaking earlier to the FBI about the shootings . . ."

"The FBI? Yeah?"

"They figure it was two brothers who did this."

Greer's gaze shifted from the TV coverage to Reznick. "What did you say?"

"The two snipers outside Yankee Stadium. The O'Keefes, apparently. But the police haven't revealed the names yet."

Greer's reddened eyes narrowed. "Who the hell are you? You seem to know a lot about what happened."

Reznick nodded. "I know because I killed the O'Keefe brothers."

Greer just stared at him. "Fuck are you talking about? You here to cause a scene?"

Reznick shook his head. "I'm going to level with you. I work on a consultancy basis for the FBI. And I was caught up in the sniper shootings this morning, like I said. And I did pursue the O'Keefe brothers and kill them."

"Who in God's name are you?"

"Like I said, my name is Jon Reznick. I'll give you the number of the FBI's assistant director who I report to if you want to verify that."

Greer took a gulp of beer. "So you walking into this bar isn't a coincidence, then, is it?"

"That's correct."

Greer went quiet.

"Your name has come up because you called the older brother of these two guys. Does the name Robert O'Keefe ring a bell?"

"Are you interviewing me here in this bar? My local bar?"

"I'm asking you a question."

"You must have the wrong guy."

Reznick shook his head. "Listen, I don't know anything about you, but I was given your name by someone I trust. I believe you know more than you're telling me. But I'm going to level with you. The stuff that happened today, the two separate sniper attacks—first Yankee Stadium and now lower Manhattan—I don't think this is over. If you know something about the O'Keefes, something that can help stop all this . . ."

Greer pinched the bridge of his nose. "Look, nice meeting you, thanks for the beer, but I've got a few things to do today."

Reznick shrugged. "I can put in a call and get the Feds to come in here, and we'll take you back to Manhattan, and we'll begin asking questions the official way. You know the drill, right?"

"You're bullshitting."

Reznick shook his head. "I can see you're a decent guy. On the level. A guy who's as appalled as any right-thinking person about what happened today." He took out his wallet and handed Greer his FBI ID. "This is real. And so am I."

Greer closed his eyes for a few moments as if trying to comprehend what was happening.

"I just want to talk. And find out what you know. There's no hidden agenda. No ulterior motive. I just want answers."

"Who sent you?"

"No one sent me. I got your number from Robert O'Keefe and made the connection. You seem to be finding this difficult, Jimmy. It doesn't have to be. But if you want, I can make your life very difficult if you don't cooperate."

"How do I know I can trust you?"

"You don't. I do freelance work for the FBI. And I know you're ex-NYPD. We just talk, no notes, no nothing."

"I don't know."

"What don't you know? The O'Keefes are killing cops on the streets of New York. Picking them off one by one. What is there to know?"

Reznick's cell phone rang. He took it out of his pocket, hoping it would be his daughter saying she had gotten back to her apartment. But the number was Meyerstein's.

"Jon, there will be a chopper there in forty minutes to pick you up."

"Got it. Martha, hold the line for a second." Reznick covered the mouthpiece and reached out to Greer. "You want to check my credentials? That's the FBI assistant director on the line right now. Here's your chance to confirm what I'm telling you."

Greer shook his head. "You're good."

Reznick moved his hand away from the mouthpiece. "I'll be waiting."

Meyerstein said, "Is that the cop, the one you were telling me about?"

"Yup. Gotta go." He ended the call and put the phone away. "Listen, I'll be out of here in forty minutes. I want you to tell me what you know. As I said, the Feds can come get you and take you back to Manhattan on the chopper that's picking me up in thirty-nine minutes."

"This is pretty irregular, how you're going about this."

"I'm a pretty irregular guy. So, let's cut the bull. Why did you call Robert O'Keefe? And why did the second call come not from you but from the US Department of Justice?"

Greer sighed and cocked his head. "Let's go somewhere quieter. I can tell you what you need to know."

Sixteen

Camila Perez felt a sense of relief as she stepped off the train and onto the platform at Atlantic Terminal, Brooklyn. It had been an hour-long journey from Hempstead. But she was glad to get away from the gang-bangers outside her neighborhood diner. The call had shaken her up. Their presence was unsettling. Terrifying. She thought they were trying to unnerve her by issuing veiled threats. But the cold, hard fact that couldn't be denied was that they had wormed their way into her life as well as Leon's. They had control over both of them.

The more she thought about it, the more she could see her life was coming apart at the seams.

Perez headed down the stifling main drag to the Armory bar. Her shirt was sticking to her back by the time she arrived. She was glad to get inside and feel the cool air on her skin. It felt good to be enjoying the anonymity and proximity to the city. It was a buzzier, more cosmopolitan atmosphere in the bar, a world away from her day-to-day life out on Long Island. The drudgery of twelve-hour night shifts at her JFK customs post meant she rarely got to see Leon, who worked in Manhattan. Today was a rare day off for her, but not for him. He was probably working flat out because of the terrible events in Manhattan. Probably why he hadn't called.

She wondered if she had been too quick to jump on the train, especially after the eerie appearance of the two goons. But she was concerned that Leon would worry if she canceled. She didn't want that.

She ordered a Bloody Mary at the bar and took her drink to the garden at the back. The scent of lavender bushes wafted in the balmy early-evening air. A few couples were already enjoying their drinks.

Perez sat down alone at a table and sipped her drink. The cool taste felt good. She felt the alcohol going straight to her head. Her mind again flashed back to the MS-13 gang members outside the diner. She sometimes wondered if she shouldn't just move on. The Leon she knew was kind, funny, and smart. And he was, despite his addictions and bad life choices, at his core, a good man. But she wondered if she shouldn't just go to the Feds herself to tell them what she knew, and to hell with the consequences. Ask for protective custody. For help for Leon.

But in her heart she knew that if she did that, the men he'd gotten tangled up with would find her and kill her. Leon knew too much; so did she. If she changed jobs, they would find her. The gang had people who had access to classified information. Friends, family, and associates. It was just a matter of exerting some pressure on an individual, and someone would give her up. It worked every time.

And Leon . . . what he had done was a federal offense. He would go to jail if anyone found out. And even in jail—actually, particularly if he was in jail—they could get to him. Kill him.

Perez sipped her drink, trying her best to relax. Her cell phone rang. She wondered if it was Leon saying he was going to be late. She had half expected that would be the case. After the tragedy in Manhattan, that would be understandable. She checked the caller ID. It was her mother, back in Tijuana.

"Mama," she said. "How are you?"

"I'm OK, *mija*. Just missing you. Are you OK, honey?"

"I'm fine, Mama. I'm safe."

"I'm watching the news. About New York. It's so terrible what's happened. It's breaking my heart, all these dead police. I can't bear it."

"I know, Mama. It's shocking."

"Who could have done that?"

"Bad people, Mama. That's who."

"Well, the bad people won't get into the country with you on duty."

Perez fought back tears.

"God bless the families of the fallen NYPD officers tonight," her mother said. "I will pray for them. I hope you will too, Camila."

"I will, Mama. I will light a candle for each of them. I promise."

"May God watch over you, my darling girl. I miss you."

"I miss you too, Mama. How is Papa?"

Camila's mother sighed. "You know how he is. He's trying his best to make his business work. But I'm afraid our savings are getting lower and lower."

"Why don't you come back to America?"

"Your father is a proud man. He needs to be near his family, you know that. His father and brother need him. And I can't leave him here. I don't want to do that. I love your father very much."

Perez felt tears spill down her face. "I know you do. I love you, Mama." Her cell phone vibrated, indicating another call waiting. "Mama, I've got to go. I think Leon's calling me."

"Leon? Good. Well, take good care of yourself, Camila. Love you."

Perez hung up and picked up the waiting call. "Hey," she said, "how are you?"

A sigh answered her. "Not so good."

Perez's heart sank. Leon's voice sounded strained. She sensed that he was going to call off their date. "Does it have to do with what happened today? Yankee Stadium?"

"Yeah . . . a lot of crazy stuff going on. And there are two more dead cops down near Wall Street."

"I didn't know about that."

"Yeah, it's a crazy day. So, look, I'm just calling to say I'm really sorry, but I won't be able to make it tonight. I thought I could maybe manage, but things are really bad here right now."

Perez wondered if she should tell Leon about her encounter with the gangbangers. But she didn't want to give him something else to worry about. "How are you physically? Do you have your medication?"

"Do you want to keep it down?"

"Sorry, I just want to make sure you can get through the day OK."

"I'll manage, don't worry. But I really need to get back to work. Unprecedented day. Maybe the worst in the city since 9/11."

"So sad. Who could have done this?"

"I can't say. But it's not good."

"I understand. You've got work to do. Bad people to find."

"It's not good timing. I should've called earlier. Are you there already?"

Perez dabbed her eyes. He sounded strung out. "Yeah, I just got here. But it's fine. I'll get a train back, I'm good."

"Look, I'll make it up to you."

"You have nothing to make up, Leon. You have a job to do. And I wouldn't have it any other way."

"How about you?"

"How about me?"

"Your work. Are you busy?"

"You know how it is, just the usual the last few nights. People trying to hide crack cocaine wrapped in cellophane in lots of creative places."

"Way too much information," he said, laughing.

Perez smiled. She loved his laugh. It was the same uninhibited laugh her father had. "And don't get me started on the white guy I stopped, flying back from Cancún with twenty Ecstasy tablets in his ass."

"That's just gross, stop!"

It was Perez's turn to laugh. She sipped more of her drink. "Anyway, that's my life right now. It's a work in progress, you could say."

"I'm not helping your social life either."

"When will I see you next? I'm working seven nights solid starting tomorrow."

"That's tough," he said. "How about next weekend? My parents said we could use their place in Montauk. We could go out Friday and stay till Monday. Make it a long weekend."

Perez thought that sounded fantastic. She loved the East End of Long Island. East Hampton, Southampton, Montauk, Sag Harbor. She felt as if she could breathe there, far away from the grime and filth of the city, or even the dreariness of Hempstead. "Are you sure?"

"Positive."

"That works. I'm off from Wednesday until the following Tuesday, time off for covering emergency shifts."

"Montauk it is. It's gonna be great. And I'll make today up to you."

Perez took a large gulp of her cocktail. "What time are you working till tonight?"

"I'm really not sure."

"It's entirely up to you, but since I'm already close to your apartment, I could head to your place and stay there tonight."

"I'd . . . I'd love that, but we're gonna be working nonstop on this, as you can imagine."

"Look, I've got a key. I'm in Gowanus. I'll make us something nice to eat. I'll pick up a few things at Whole Foods. A late supper kind of thing. What do you say?"

"Camila, I can't make any promises. But that sounds great. Let's pencil in ten o'clock."

"Deal. Stay safe, Leon. I love you."

Seventeen

The salty air was wafting in off the sea, and the early-evening sky above Sag Harbor burned orange, as Reznick and Greer headed onto the near-deserted beach after leaving the bar.

Reznick started the conversation. "So . . . tell me your story."

"I used to be NYPD, as you know," Greer said. "I got my full pension early. Very early."

"You seem pretty young to be retired."

"They said it was ill health."

"You don't seem very ill to me."

"I'm not."

"So what happened?"

Greer shook his head, staring down at the sand. "It was all fucked up, Jon. Politics."

"Tell me about your role."

"This is where it might get tricky for me."

"Tell me what you know about the O'Keefe brothers—the two who are dead, and the other one, Todd, who's alive. Enough of the bullshit."

Greer shook his head. "I can't."

"Why the hell not?"

"My lawyer got me a great deal. And I had to sign a nondisclosure agreement with the NYPD."

"I'm not interested in fucking agreements and deals. I want to know what you know. Do you understand? Otherwise, you'll be accompanying me back to Manhattan, whether you want to or not."

"I need to talk to my lawyer first."

"Are you kidding me? Eight cops are dead outside Yankee Stadium, two more in the Financial District, and maybe more to come, and you want to talk about legal agreements?"

Greer shrugged. "It's the way it is."

Reznick sighed. "Fine, make the call." He looked at his watch. "I've only got twenty-nine minutes. I want answers."

Eighteen

Meyerstein and her team were in a conference room on the twenty-sixth floor of the FBI's New York field office in lower Manhattan. She'd been glued to the live TV coverage of the sniper attacks. Now she pointed the remote control at the screen, replacing the news footage with a dead-eyed Department of Corrections photo of Todd O'Keefe.

She turned in her chair and looked around at the faces of the FBI analysts and agents at the table. Some with laptops, some taking notes, some sitting with piles of briefing notes in front of them on the huge mahogany table.

"This is a live situation which is rapidly getting out of control," she said. "Now, I've been checking up on Todd O'Keefe's FBI records, those of his brothers—the two deceased shooters—and also Charles Campbell."

Meyerstein clicked the button on the remote. Black-and-white photos showed the two dead O'Keefe brothers. "The killers. Thankfully they were brought down by none other than Jon Reznick, who was with his daughter when the initial events unfolded."

A young female behavioral analyst said, "Is he formally working for the FBI?"

Meyerstein detected a slightly arrogant tone in the young woman's voice. "He's working in an advisory capacity. It was fortunate that he was there."

The young woman said, "Forgive me a moment, Assistant Director, and I hope you don't think I'm speaking out of turn . . ."

"Speak your mind."

"Might it not have been more helpful if Reznick had taken them alive?"

An awkward silence stretched around the table. "I beg your pardon?"

"Well, surely arresting the two men would have yielded far better intelligence on what was happening and how these O'Keefes were all linked."

Meyerstein said, "Have you seen the footage where one of them points a rifle at Reznick outside a bodega? Or the other one, who aimed his rifle at innocent bystanders in a crowded subway station?"

"Yes, I have."

"And you think Reznick should have tried harder to take them alive?"

"I'm saying, with respect, that it complicates matters to have two suspects dead instead of in custody, answering our questions. Reznick's reaction was overkill."

Meyerstein shook her head. "How long have you been with the FBI?"

The young analyst blushed. "Two years and seven months."

"You're barely in the door. Give it a little longer before you start second-guessing the reactions of a man trained to protect others. That man put his life on the line to take those men down. You seriously believe that neutralizing two psychopaths who killed eight cops, including two in a chopper, could have been handled differently? You're wrong. And embarrassingly so."

The room was silent.

Meyerstein felt incredibly defensive when it came to Jon Reznick. She understood better than anyone the problems, both legal and ethical, his involvement posed for the FBI. She had lost count of the number of times she had taken flak from the Director and other senior members of the FBI executive team over Reznick's methods. She didn't disagree that he was invariably a shoot-now-and-ask-questions-later kind of operative. But in part that was due to the nature of the investigations he worked on—which were almost always incredibly fast moving, highly stressful, and extremely dangerous.

It was easy to be critical. But without Reznick's help, it was unlikely the FBI would have tackled those various threats in as direct or effective a manner. He got the job done. He was a patriot.

Meyerstein stared at the expressionless young analyst. She thought back to herself at that age. She had always listened to those far more experienced than her. Had been guided by what they knew. How they operated. What the hell was Quantico teaching its recruits these days?

She wasn't going to take any lectures from know-it-all kids fresh out of college with no real-world experience. In fact, she had *given* numerous lectures at prestigious colleges across America. But the young woman's comments reflected a new orthodoxy that Martha had noticed taking hold. It wasn't about what was right and what was wrong. It wasn't about the law. It was all about being sensitive.

She'd lost count of the number of softball approaches that seemed to be the preferred mode of law enforcement these days. "Redirection" was one—the idea of simply warning a person not to repeat their crime, and hoping they would reform. It was almost as if it wasn't about cracking down on illegal acts, but about showing a more understanding approach to law enforcement.

As a result, the organization had become less muscular, less robust, and Meyerstein increasingly felt at odds with the culture. Her decision to continue to work with Reznick was viewed with disapproval in some quarters. She knew a few people were talking behind her back about why she sanctioned someone so unpredictable. She knew because those agents she trusted, people she called friends, had told her. She had even inadvertently overheard some watercooler talk between two younger male special agents who speculated that she was having an affair with Reznick.

The implication was that she wasn't thinking straight. Letting emotion get in the way of her critical-thinking faculties. In fact, nothing was further from the truth.

Meyerstein saw exactly what Reznick brought to the table, time after time, in the most difficult and trying of investigations. And each and every time, Reznick, while crossing numerous lines, always seemed to rein things in, allowing an invaluable capability to be deployed as and when the FBI wanted it.

She looked around the table. "Let me be quite clear. If Reznick hadn't gone after the snipers, we have no idea how many more people—cops or civilians—they would have killed. There are no elegant solutions in such circumstances. Sometimes, someone has to get down and dirty. And if any of you has a problem trying to figure out what the FBI is all about, and where its loyalties lie, it's to the people of the United States of America." Meyerstein looked across at the by now sheepish-looking female analyst. "Jon Reznick is, as we speak, out on Long Island, asking questions. Questions which have not been answered. He's not killing people. He's asking questions. And you know what those questions produced? It started me looking more closely at the files on the O'Keefes. Robert O'Keefe called the FBI three months ago to warn us of a potential Aryan Brotherhood–inspired spectacle."

The carefully blank expressions on the special agents' and analysts' faces told their own story. Someone had fucked up, and each person hoped it wasn't them.

Meyerstein's gaze wandered around the table once more. "Leon."

Cortez's face drained of color.

Meyerstein looked at him. "You mind explaining something to me, Leon?"

"I'm not entirely sure what you mean."

"Really? Well, let me enlighten you. I have finally managed to get my hands on the details of Robert O'Keefe's tip, which was filed incorrectly, not tagging the O'Keefes."

"Apologies for that."

Meyerstein stared at him long and hard. "And that's that, right?"

Cortez shook his head. "Ma'am, it was an honest error."

"Leon, do you know I had to get someone to trawl through numerous other files to retrieve it? I see there is a handwritten telephone interview note. It specifically uses the phrase *Robert O'Keefe believes this is a credible threat from his brother, Todd.* Which sounds pretty clear-cut if you ask me."

Cortez nodded.

"Did you write that note?"

"Yes, I did, ma'am."

"Yet you failed to follow up on it or to enter an official report, and egregiously misfiled your notes. Would you like to explain this discrepancy?"

"This is kinda awkward." Cortez shifted in his seat. "I was informed that the DEA was handling the case, and they said an NYPD undercover cop was taken off a sensitive investigation."

Meyerstein stared across the table. "You lost me. So the DEA got an NYPD operative taken off an investigation? What investigation?"

Cortez sighed. "The NYPD had several high-level sources to protect, that's what the DEA said. They were concerned they would be compromised."

Meyerstein looked around at the others, who were also staring at Cortez. "That doesn't explain why you didn't follow up on it or write a report. Do not try and deflect on this; it won't work."

Cortez went quiet for a few moments.

"What was the name of the person in the DEA you spoke to? You got a name for the file, surely."

"Someone high up. I can't remember."

"You can't remember. Well, that is interesting."

Cortez shifted in his seat like a scolded schoolboy. "I can't explain right at this moment what my reasoning was."

Meyerstein looked around the table at the other analysts and special agents. "Can you give us a minute? I need to speak to Special Agent Cortez in private. Your job is to find Todd O'Keefe. *Before* he kills anyone else. Now! Get to it!"

The others hurriedly gathered up their papers and laptops, leaving Meyerstein and Cortez at opposite sides of the conference table.

Meyerstein looked at Cortez. She felt anger, not sympathy. This didn't look good from where she stood.

She got up and walked to the windows overlooking lower Manhattan. She saw the Freedom Tower glistening in the early-evening sun. "You need to tell me now what the hell has been going on. I'm not buying what you just told me. And your actions, from what you've said, don't match your story." She turned to face Cortez. "Well?"

Cortez leaned back in his seat and shook his head. "What I said about the DEA is true."

"Are we supposed to take your word for it? We have no file, no notes."

"That's correct. I was told to just leave it alone, and that was that."

Meyerstein began to pick through this revelation. It was beyond belief that this was only now being unearthed. "Leon, I don't think you understand the gravity of today's events. Eight cops died this morning, two this afternoon. Ten cops dead! In your city!"

Cortez sighed, staring at his notes.

"Chopper blown out of the sky. You were warned about the serious threat posed by the O'Keefes. You spoke to Robert O'Keefe. Do you understand the optics of this? How it will look? It's really bad!"

"I don't know . . . I don't think I've been thinking straight for a while."

Meyerstein looked at Cortez. His skin seemed waxy with sweat. She sensed something was wrong. Not only with the procedures he hadn't followed, but also with his demeanor. "What are you talking about?"

Cortez cleared his throat and reached for the glass of water in front of him. He took a couple of sips. "I've been sick. I think the pressure has been building up. I can't stand it anymore. I swear to God, I want out!"

Meyerstein walked over to the young agent, pulled up a chair, and sat down next to him. She looked into his eyes. They were bloodshot, pupils like pinpricks. Beads of sweat were forming on his forehead.

"I feel sick. I think I need to see a doctor."

Meyerstein could see with her own eyes that Cortez was genuinely not well. Was it a fever?

"Sick, what I've done. What I've become. I'm not thinking straight. I've got constant pain and cramps."

"Leon, what the hell are you talking about? You sound like a hypochondriac all of a sudden."

"I've worked surveillance. I put in a lot of hours. I don't know whether I'm coming or going half the time. And I can't seem to relax. I'm in pain. All the time."

"Pain? You keep saying you're in pain. You mean mental pain? Pain from what?"

Cortez picked up the glass of water with a shaking hand. He took a couple of gulps. He returned the glass to the table. His tremor was clearly noticeable.

"Leon, be very clear with me now: you either talk to me or I will be compelled to speak to the FBI's Office of Professional Responsibility. You know what they do, right?"

Cortez rubbed his eyes.

"They'll investigate your conduct. It's serious stuff. They do not mess around. And if they find that your misconduct was serious enough, or intentional, you could be charged with a crime. So, do you want to tell me what the hell is going on? Or do you want to speak to a lawyer?"

Cortez closed his eyes in anguish.

"Don't make it harder for yourself, Leon. If you want a full-blown investigation into every aspect of your work and your life, fine, that can be arranged. My advice? Talk to me."

"I want to be open."

Meyerstein shrugged.

"I need to talk about this. I've been holding all this in. Christ, I'm in so much pain."

"Talk to me about this pain. How did it start?"

Cortez buried his head in his hands.

"How did this, whatever *this* is, begin?"

"It began . . . I was on a Joint Task Force, investigating gangs, cross-border trafficking, with the NYPD. We were investigating the O'Keefes. And that's when it began, about a year ago."

"When what began?"

"I was on a stakeout. It was dark. And I tripped and fell down some stairs. I was put on some goddamn prescription painkillers because I had injured my arm."

Meyerstein recognized in a split second what the problem was and why he was in pain. "You're addicted to painkillers?"

Cortez closed his eyes. "I feel so ashamed."

"Leon, if you have medical issues, we can help you with that. We'll get you better. But first, we need to establish the facts about Robert O'Keefe's call. Do you understand?"

"I feel like I've become another person. I was working undercover a lot. I wasn't sleeping. I seemed to be working morning, noon, and night. That's how it all started with the O'Keefes, how I got drawn into their orbit."

"Slow down, Leon."

"I got to know what they were up to. But I had no idea they were going to do this. I feel sick. And I feel guilty. Guilty for what's happened. Guilty for what I've put people through. I'm responsible."

"Responsible for what? What exactly are you getting at?"

Cortez's eyes were filling with tears. He took off his jacket and rolled up his sleeves. His arms were covered in track marks, some scabbed over. "It's not just painkillers. Do you see what I'm saying?"

Meyerstein stared at the scabs and the marks where the needles had been. "How long?"

"A few months. I started off using the painkillers. I quickly became addicted to them. And then I stole some heroin from an evidence safe."

Meyerstein felt sick and shaken up at his revelations. She wondered where this confession was going to end up.

"But when that H ran out, I needed more."

Meyerstein felt a terrible emptiness within her. She was struggling to take it all in.

"No easier mark than a junkie cop, is there? I started getting followed. And then I was approached."

"Approached by who?"

"People who knew who I was. They didn't identify themselves, but there were tattoos on their necks. MS-13. They showed me photographs of me snorting lines at a dealer's house in Queens. They assured me they could get me a never-ending supply. But they wanted something in return."

"Are you kidding me? You're an FBI agent. You should know how we deal with such things."

Cortez shook his head. "It's not that simple."

"How is it not that simple?"

"There weren't threats. Just quietly spoken, carefully chosen phrases. They said it would be best for me and my family if I could ensure the O'Keefe brothers were left alone. 'They're our friends,' they said."

Meyerstein began to see some connections. "And so, when Robert O'Keefe contacted you with his serious concerns about his psychotic brothers, you took the statement, but then you buried it."

Cortez nodded. "I know it sounds bad."

"You're damn right it sounds bad. What else?"

"The Aryan Brotherhood, despite their race affiliations, has a loose alliance with MS-13. The Mexican Mafia."

"Tell me something I don't know. I want the full, unvarnished story. Who else knows about these threats? What about your fiancée?"

"Camila is innocent. She's trying to get me off the drugs."

"Leon, I'd like you to hand over your gun for safekeeping until this matter is resolved."

Cortez took off his gun and slid it across the table to her. "What about my badge?"

"That's up to the OPR. For now, I'm going to put this in the field office main safe. At least for now."

Cortez nodded, staring at the floor. "I just wanted to say, ma'am, that I'm truly sorry."

Meyerstein just stared at him, feeling nothing but contempt.

Nineteen

Reznick was deep in conversation with Greer on the beach in Sag Harbor when his cell phone rang. It was Meyerstein.

"Jon, I got something," she said.

She gave him a terse update. It centered on a face-to-face conversation with Special Agent Leon Cortez. It hardly seemed possible.

Reznick looked at his watch. "This just gets worse. The Aryan Brotherhood and MS-13. Where's the chopper?"

"Ten minutes out. I just wanted you to know."

"Appreciate the heads-up."

"Stay safe, Jon."

Reznick ended the call.

"That your boss?" Greer said.

Reznick nodded. "Well, the person I report to," he said. He took a couple of minutes to explain what he'd heard. "Does all that sound probable? Or even credible?"

Greer said, "I might be able to help you here. I know Cortez."

"You do?"

Greer nodded, shielding his eyes from the setting sun. "We worked surveillance on gang and drug task forces over the last few years. Yeah, I know the kid."

"What was he like?"

"He was very good. Diligent. Serious. Steady. But . . ."

"But what?"

"What you told me doesn't surprise me."

"What doesn't surprise you?"

"The addiction."

"I don't understand. You just said he was diligent."

"Six or seven months ago, I caught him passed out. It was a Joint Task Force investigation—FBI, DEA, NYPD—and he was slumped in the back of an unmarked car."

"Are you serious?"

"The guy was doing heroin."

"Was this reported?"

Greer sighed. "Look, I didn't want to get the kid in trouble. I just told my boss I didn't want to work with him. And that was that."

"Jimmy, we don't believe this is simply about the O'Keefes or one rogue agent."

"I think you're getting closer to the true picture. The big picture."

Reznick said, "Tell me what you know. What is the big picture?"

"Look . . . this is difficult for me. I signed a nondisclosure agreement. My lawyer says this would open up future actions against me. I need my pension."

"Fuck your pension, you're talking to me. And only me. Ten cops dead? Tell me what you know. Don't give me any nondisclosure agreement bullshit."

Greer stopped on the beach, hands thrust into the pockets of his jeans. "The O'Keefes—all three of them—were low- to mid-level drug smugglers across the United States. We were keeping an eye on the whole operation. The drugs came up through Mexico and then connected with the Aryan Brotherhood of Texas."

"That's better. I'm starting to get a feel for the big picture."

"The ABT in turn used their members in that area—Houston, Dallas, Corpus Christi—as mules, including the O'Keefes, who frequently came up to New York. But this goes beyond just a joint operation smuggling methamphetamine and heroin. This was so much more. And that's what you really need to understand."

"Jimmy, you're killing me. What else do you know?"

"This all comes down to one guy. Charlie Campbell."

"The O'Keefes' stepfather?"

Greer nodded. "He was a top guy in the Aryan Brotherhood. A player. When he was released seventeen years ago—and by the way, I have no fucking idea how they let him out of jail; he still had a twenty-nine-year stretch ahead of him . . ."

"Hang on, so Campbell should never have been released?"

"Check the guy's record. He was given forty years. He served eleven years."

Reznick stopped walking as he contemplated the ramifications of releasing someone like Campbell. But also the chances of being released with that kind of criminal record. They began to walk on. "OK, so are you saying, and I don't want to put words in your mouth, that you believe he was being protected?"

"He was an asset. A major-league informant. And so much more. I probably don't know the half of it."

"Tell me about the half you do know."

Greer shook his head. "I had some serious run-ins with the Feds in New York, just in the last couple of months. We'd been working together, but all of a sudden the task force seemed like it was a constant battle, and I didn't like how they kept on interfering in our intelligence operation."

"The field office?"

"Yeah. We were getting stalled left, right, and center. It got to the stage where we were just going ahead and ignoring the Feds, and it was all sort of shit after that."

"What do you mean?"

"I suddenly had some disciplinary black marks against me, complaints piling up—anonymous complaints. It ground me down. Department of Justice lawyers were suddenly questioning whether NYPD and the New York AG had any state-level case against Campbell and the O'Keefes or whether we needed to hand it all over to the Feds—who, as I mentioned, were showing zero interest in pursuing these guys. Eventually, my lawyer made a deal to get my pension and full benefits early, just so long as I kept my head down and shut the hell up."

"How did it all get so crazy, Jimmy?"

"Cortez was a weak link in the chain. But he wasn't the main problem in the scheme of things. Campbell was involved with the Mexican Mafia and MS-13. But those mean motherfuckers would have tortured and killed him if they realized he was a government asset."

"American government asset?"

"Got it."

"Tell me about Campbell's arrest and sudden death, which seems to have sparked this."

"Happened about a week after I was moved out. NYPD undercover gang officers were furious that Campbell was still free despite the great case they had against him and the O'Keefe boys, and they decided to move against him, without the FBI's or the DOJ's say-so. Without the DEA's say-so. And the bastard was put in some choke hold, was struggling like a madman, and the fuck died. I for one won't shed any tears over the bastard."

"And from there?"

"And from there, all the rest followed. Complete shitstorm."

"If I told you that members of the Mexican Mafia made veiled threats to Special Agent Cortez, what would you say?"

"The Aryan Brotherhood and Mexican Mafia are businesses. They need to make money. And any threat to that is a threat to them. But also, Jon, I don't know if you know this about Campbell, but he was a regular visitor to Mexico once he got out of prison. DEA photographed him with several cartel associates. He was running an operation across the border, undoubtedly with the O'Keefes."

Reznick was starting to get an inkling of the multiple strands and complexities of the investigation. "So if the task force investigation led to arresting Campbell, the primary conduit into and out of Mexico, the cartel's go-between with the Brotherhood would be gone."

"That's just the beginning. He was also running guns into Mexico and the US."

"Guns? Are you kidding me?"

"AK-47s. But—and I heard it from a CIA guy who was on a joint terrorism task force a couple years back—Campbell was also tight with the Agency."

"The CIA?"

"Langley had operatives who trained the Mexican military, federal police—they exchanged information, intelligence, but also had links with those at the top of the Sinaloa Cartel."

Reznick stared at Greer. He was only now starting to understand exactly how Campbell had gotten away with so much for so long. "Campbell was a strategic intelligence asset—is that what you're saying?"

"Precisely. And he was protected. By the cartel, but also by the CIA. The Sinaloa tipped off the Agency and the DEA about drugs being trafficked by other cartels, and they were left alone. Friend of mine on the force told me the Department of Justice made sure the FBI was out of the loop. And Cortez was a useful idiot in the whole complete mess."

Reznick ran his hands over his face, trying to get a handle on a seriously fucked-up situation.

"Charlie Campbell was essentially a logistics coordinator for the Mexican Mafia and the AB," Greer said. "But the CIA knew this. They had their fingers in many pies. Mexican politicians, police, army, cartel. They were pulling the strings. And the end result was all that junk flooding into the United States. Methamphetamine, heroin, and cocaine. Tons of it. They left Campbell alone. Why? Campbell was supplying intelligence to them. Opening up contacts. Secret back channels to and from Mexico."

"This is crazy."

Reznick looked at Greer, who was facing him, the beach stretching behind him. He could see, plain as day, that the ex-cop was telling the truth. The unvarnished truth.

Suddenly, Greer's face exploded, blood and brains everywhere. The crack of a rifle shot echoed in the distance.

The ex-cop collapsed in the sand, his body lifeless.

Reznick instinctively threw himself on the ground and scrambled for cover. He turned around. Farther down the beach, about half a mile away, a sniper rifle was aimed straight at him.

Twenty

Bullets peppered the sand, dangerously close.

Reznick dove for the cover of nearby sand dunes. He hunkered down. A dull *phut* sounded as a shot tore into the long, sandy grass. He was breathing hard. Another bullet. And another. Then nothing.

He waited, not daring to move.

Reznick couldn't just keep wondering how long the gunman would hang around. He scrambled up the dunes and peered over the top. In the distance he saw what looked like a thickset white man getting into a black SUV. The car sped off.

Reznick ran back down the beach and crouched over the dead cop's bloodied body. "Oh shit, Jimmy."

The sound of chopper blades echoed in the distance. He turned and saw the FBI helicopter swooping in low as it prepared to land on the beach.

He looked up, frantically waving his arms. "Here! Here!"

Reznick felt the downdraft from the rotor blades. The sand was whipping up in his face. He screwed up his eyes and turned his back on the chopper. He felt a terrible chasm begin to open within him. He was responsible. He wondered if he could have prevented the killing. Was it just bad timing? Had the sniper been keeping watch on Greer, or had someone followed Reznick and he'd led them straight to Greer? Was the killer Todd O'Keefe?

His mind began to race ahead as the chopper set down. He realized he couldn't leave Greer's still-warm body just lying on the beach. It would soon be swarming with cops and God knows who else. He needed to get Greer's body out of there. Besides, the bullets that had killed him could also be identified by the medical examiner during an autopsy.

He hunkered down for a few more moments as the helicopter landed. The door opened. The guy inside signaled him toward the chopper.

Reznick slid one hand under Greer's torn, bloodied head and one under his legs, and carried the body. The Fed inside the chopper nodded, pulling the body inside.

"Jon Reznick?" the Fed asked.

Reznick nodded. "Yeah. We need to get out of here, son."

"Who is he?"

"Ex-NYPD cop, Jimmy Greer. We are not leaving him here. Under any circumstances."

The Fed nodded. "Agreed."

Reznick slumped in a seat and buckled himself up, a million thoughts running through his head as he strapped Greer's lifeless body in beside him. The Fed adjusted his headset and strapped himself in on the other side.

The pilot leaned back and handed Reznick a headset. He put it on.

The pilot's voice filled his ears. "I was just asked to pick you up here and take you back to Manhattan. What the hell is this?"

"This is a dead ex-NYPD officer."

"That's not my problem."

"It is now. Listen, a sniper just took this guy out. He got in a black SUV and sped off. I want you to find the bastard that did this. Can you try and track him?"

"Negative," the pilot said. "My orders are very specific. To pick you up, and only you, and take you straight back to Manhattan."

"I'll get you the authorization. Get me Martha Meyerstein, patch her through onto the headset. I'll speak to her. We don't know if the guy in the SUV is going after anyone else."

"Roger that. Stand by."

The helicopter took off, banked in a southerly direction before heading due west. A few moments later, Meyerstein's voice crackled through the headset. "Jon, what happened?"

"The cop—the undercover cop, Greer, I was speaking to—has just been taken out. Long-range sniper."

"Are you kidding me?"

"Negative. Happened on the beach here in Sag Harbor."

"Copy that."

Reznick sighed. "Martha, the guy escaped in an SUV. Black SUV. He's three, maybe four, minutes ahead of us. But we should be able to catch him. I want the go-ahead."

"Jon, this is coming at us from all angles. I think we should leave that to an FBI SWAT team."

"It'll take too much time to get them out here. We don't know what this guy is up to. We don't know if it's Todd O'Keefe. No fucking idea."

"Let's do it."

"Thanks. Martha, I've got Greer's body here in the chopper. I didn't want him lying on the beach."

"What?"

"We're dealing with a concerted attempt to kill cops. I want authorization to take him with us."

"You've got the go-ahead from me. Get him to Manhattan, we'll get him to the mortuary. This is too much for one day."

"Tell me about it."

"One final thing, Jon. Probably seems incidental after what's just happened, but did you find out anything at all from Greer?"

Reznick relayed their conversation. "Charlie Campbell was being protected. He was a government asset. And he was also linked with the Mexican Mafia. I'm telling you, this is fucked up. And it ain't over."

"I got that, Jon. I'll get the backup you need."

"Whatever it takes."

The pilot came back on. "He'll probably want to get onto the turnpike, and then head to the Montauk Highway."

"Let's get there. I want that bastard taken down."

The chopper veered back to the south over the turnpike, flying low. They scoured the roads below, mile after mile, but no vehicle matched the description Reznick had given. The chopper swooped low as it skirted the back road toward Bridgehampton.

Reznick swore. "Nothing!"

"He could have headed east in the direction of Montauk. Then again, he could've gone west toward Southampton."

"Try Southampton. That's also the road back to Manhattan."

The pilot nodded. "Copy that."

The chopper veered west and then flew directly over the westbound traffic on Montauk Highway.

Reznick scanned the road for black SUVs.

"Could be anywhere," the pilot said.

"Copy that. Let's just follow this road. And if we get nothing, hopefully the cops will be able to catch him."

Reznick wondered how the hell they weren't seeing anything. Had the driver changed vehicles? That was a possibility. But as it was, there was no trace. It was as if the car had disappeared into the affluent

Hampton oceanfront communities or adjacent verdant farmland, gone forever.

The earpiece crackled to life. "Jon, it's Martha. We have a visual."

Reznick clenched his fist. "Copy that."

"Our forensics guys have been looking over surveillance cameras in and around Sag Harbor. They've located the SUV. It's a Mercedes, a rental. Hired by a Bobby Campbell."

"Campbell?"

"Yeah. Brother of Charlie Campbell. Been based down in Florida for about twenty years."

"Location?"

"That's the thing. The SUV is approaching a house located at 253 Meadow Lane, Southampton. Ultra-exclusive oceanfront community."

Reznick tapped the pilot on the shoulder. "You get that?"

"Copy that," he said, and pointed the chopper directly to nearby Southampton.

Reznick said, "What else do I need to know?"

"The house is owned by Tom Friedkin, none other than the attorney general of New York."

"You've got to be kidding me."

"Friedkin was the guy who prosecuted Charlie Campbell and his brother all those years ago."

"Out for revenge?"

The chopper was swooping dangerously low over huge mansions by the water, right on the beach.

Meyerstein said, "That and helping the O'Keefes to carry out numerous headline-grabbing spectacles."

Reznick tapped the pilot on the shoulder. "Land at the rear of the house."

"Roger that."

Reznick adjusted the headset. "Martha, one final request."

"What?"

"Get the number for the Friedkin home, call and tell them to hide. I'm on my way."

"Good luck, Jon. SWAT team is en route."

"It's going to be too late for that."

Twenty-One

Reznick looked at the Fed in the back of the chopper. "You got a rifle?"

"A rifle?"

"Simple question. Have you got a rifle on board?"

The Fed nodded. He reached under the seat and popped open a metal gun box. "Sir, I don't know if this is part of the orders we were given."

"Assistant Director Meyerstein has given the go-ahead to intercept the shooter in the SUV."

The Fed handed Reznick the high-powered rifle. "It's only supposed to be myself or the pilot who can use that, sir."

Reznick checked the sights, then clipped on the magazine. Flicked off the safety. He adjusted his headset. "Pilot, get me within two hundred yards at a height of seventy-five yards! I need to see what's going on."

"Stand by." The pilot maneuvered the chopper.

Suddenly, Reznick had the sprawling mansion in his sights.

"Copy that. Hold it steady!" Reznick leaned forward as the chopper jolted back and forward. The pilot was struggling to keep control in the offshore wind gusts. Reznick lined up the rifle crosshairs on the black SUV that was parked on a gravel driveway out the back. "Fuck!

The bastard's here! Inside! Get me around the far side. The beach side, see if I can spot him."

The chopper maneuvered again to the front of the house. Reznick looked through the crosshairs of the rifle. He thought he saw some movement in a room at the front. It looked like a woman and two children cowering. But no sign of the shooter.

"Put us down in the rear garden!" Reznick ordered. "I'm going in."

He handed the rifle to the Fed. "You're coming with me."

"Shouldn't we wait for backup, sir?"

Reznick took off his headset and placed it under his seat. "No time. You coming?"

The agent was in his thirties, but he seemed like he was out of his comfort zone. "Sure." The Fed took off his headset as he followed Reznick off the chopper and onto the lush grass in the sprawling rear garden.

Reznick hand-signaled his intent. "You go around and cover the front door. Whatever you do, make sure he doesn't leave the property. I'll do this side of the house."

The Fed nodded and headed down the path with his rifle as Reznick covered him.

Reznick approached the rear of the house, his trusty 9mm Beretta in his hand. He peered into the kitchen window. There was some movement down the hall. He looked down the side of the house and saw a window open. It looked like a downstairs bathroom. He headed down the concrete path.

The sound of a woman's frightened voice came from inside. "Please, they're just children! You're scaring them!"

Reznick edged closer.

A man's voice drawled, "Where is your husband, lady?"

"I don't know," Mrs. Friedkin wailed.

"I don't fucking believe you. So you better remember real quick," the guy roared. "Do you know who I am?"

The woman wailed louder.

"Your fucking husband is who I'm after, not you or your kids. Where the fuck is he?"

Mrs. Friedkin cried, "Please . . . don't hurt them! Take my watch. We've got money."

"Oh, I know you do."

Reznick slid the gun into his waistband and pulled himself up to the window. He climbed inside, dropping down onto the tiled floor.

The sound of children screaming. "Mommy, Mommy!"

Reznick edged out of the bathroom.

The man's voice boomed. "Tell them to shut the fuck up!"

"Please, they're just children!"

Reznick got down on his knees and crawled toward the commotion. He had no way of knowing where the intruder was.

The man roared, "Who the fuck is that? Out front! I saw someone!"

Reznick realized the intruder had spotted the young Fed. He got to his feet, crept down the hallway, gun at the ready. The voices sounded like they were in the room adjacent. To the right.

Slowly he peered around the corner.

Mrs. Friedkin was staring wide-eyed at him. Her eyes darted to the right as if to indicate where the sniper was.

Reznick nodded to acknowledge. He pressed his finger to his lips to indicate not to say a word. He eased forward. The woman's eyes were glassy. Terrified. He took a step closer. He turned and entered the room, 9mm Beretta drawn.

A huge tattooed white guy was standing in an alcove, arm wrapped around one of the little girls, rifle pointed at her head. "Well, looks like we've got company."

"Put the gun down, Campbell!" Reznick said.

The guy began to grin and exploded with laughter. "How do you know my name?"

"FBI, put down the weapon."

The girl began to wail. "Mommy!"

Campbell pressed the rifle tighter to her head. "She gets it, tough guy, if you so much as look at me the wrong way. Don't think I won't. People like this mean zero to me."

Reznick trained the Beretta on the guy's forehead, finger on the trigger. Senses switched on. He blocked out everything apart from Bobby Campbell and the girl. "This doesn't have to happen. Just drop the gun."

Campbell began to laugh and turned to look at the mother. "What do you take me—"

Reznick squeezed the trigger twice. A double tap to the forehead. Deafening gunshots. Blood and brains splattered the wall and the little girl's face and her pink dress. The smell of cordite rose as the dead man collapsed, arms entangled with the screaming girl, pinning her to the ground.

Reznick rushed forward and pulled the terrified girl out of the bloody clutches of Charlie Campbell's dead brother.

Twenty-Two

It was all over by the time a couple of FBI SWAT teams pulled up on the gravel drive of the New York attorney general's sprawling estate.

Reznick quickly briefed the team leader on what had happened. The family was bundled into the back of one of the SWAT vehicles and driven away to a safe location. The second SWAT team secured the scene until the cops and medical examiner could arrive.

Reznick and the other Fed got back in the chopper and put on their headsets. He looked at the bloodied body of Greer, still strapped into the back seat. He looked at the Fed, who was ashen faced. "You OK?"

"Yeah, I'm fine."

"I think he spotted you out front. Lucky he didn't take a potshot at you."

The Fed nodded, hands trembling. "I'll radio ahead to get the medical examiner's people to pick Greer's body up."

Reznick clasped his shoulder. "It's OK, man, it's over."

They sat in silence for a few minutes as the chopper headed back to Manhattan before Reznick's headset crackled to life.

"Jon," said Meyerstein, "I just heard from the SWAT team what happened. Are you OK?"

Reznick turned and looked at the Fed, who was now smiling in relief. "We're fine."

"You're having a helluva Fourth of July."

"I've had better. Martha, it's clear Charlie Campbell's brother was in on this. The plan has been coordinated. And we're talking inside knowledge. This guy, after taking out Greer, was headed to find the attorney general and kill him."

"Too bad his wife and kids were home."

"They're shaken up big time, as you can imagine. Seriously traumatized."

Meyerstein sighed. "We believe now that there has been an intelligence leak or breach—probably within the FBI, thanks to Cortez—which effectively identified Greer's whereabouts."

"If this gets out, the shit will hit the fan. You know that, right?"

"Trust me, I know what the fallout will be. We're looking into Cortez's family. Trying to find out if his fiancée or acquaintances have been compromised in some way because of him, or if it's just him."

Reznick shook his head. "Tell me about Greer. Does he have a family?"

"He's married, two kids."

"Jesus Christ, Martha. What the hell?"

"I know. It's bad. And it just seems to be getting worse."

"This is not over. Listen to me, I don't think it's just FBI. Greer mentioned the DEA and the CIA. They're all wrapped up in this sordid piece of shit. Government agencies are facilitating this by their actions, or inactions. They're turning a blind eye here, there, and everywhere. And all because of the supposed big picture."

Meyerstein remained silent.

"It's disgusting. If the public knew that this had happened, that the O'Keefes were allowed to go ahead with this attack on the city, they would be descending on the FBI HQ and burning it to the fucking ground."

"Jon, that's enough! We don't know for sure where the leak came from."

"We know you had a rotten agent. And that's just the start."

"I get it, Jon. And we'll deal with that another day. We've got a real-time situation here."

Reznick sighed and adjusted the headset microphone. "What's the latest?"

"We have analysts trying to piece this together. We believe that Midtown Manhattan is where Todd O'Keefe might emerge."

Reznick's stomach tightened. "Are you kidding me? Well, that's just great. Midtown on the Fourth of July. Just great."

"How long will it take you to get there?"

Reznick looked at his watch. "Twenty minutes, give or take."

Meyerstein sighed.

"Martha, the cover is darkness. Theaters will be mobbed. Tens of thousands of visitors. Bars. Restaurants. Times Square is nuts at the best of times. After everything that's happened, it'll be perfect. Creating chaos. Picking off cops in the middle of New York. I can see that. A lot of planning and logistics have gone into this. This is not happening off the cuff."

"I have a major team looking into this. But I'm going to get them to trawl Greer's files and reach out to the DEA."

"What's the DEA saying?"

"We're still waiting to hear an official line from them."

"Check Greer's cell phone records. He was using that to communicate with Robert O'Keefe before he was sidelined. There might be something there."

"We're already speaking to the NYPD on this. There'll be an FBI vehicle to pick you up when you land."

Reznick looked out of the chopper window at Queens below. In the far distance he saw planes landing at JFK. They were getting closer to Manhattan. But not fast enough.

Twenty-Three

Todd O'Keefe dropped the minivan at a junkyard owned by a longtime associate of the Brand. It was crushed and pummeled as he watched. It felt satisfying, destroying the physical evidence. But his work in the city wasn't done. Not by a long stretch.

The junkyard owner drove him to a dive bar six blocks away. "Stay safe, bro," he said. "You'll get a visit from a kid in a few minutes. He's one of us."

O'Keefe thanked the guy and headed inside. He looked around the dark interior of the bar. It was deserted. It felt gothic, faded leather booths dotted around. The smell of stale cigarettes and cheap whiskey. At the far end of the bar sat the obligatory jukebox and pool table. He got himself a beer and headed over to one of the booths in the far corner.

O'Keefe sat down and took a drink. He savored the cold lager. He'd earned it. A few minutes later, a skinhead sauntered in wearing a backpack. The kid ordered a Heineken and walked over to the booth.

"You mind if I sit down?" he said.

"Go right ahead."

O'Keefe couldn't place his accent. He sounded West Coast, perhaps.

"Real hot out there today, huh?"

"You got that right," O'Keefe said.

"Crazy stuff going on up in the Bronx, I heard."

"You from around here, son?"

The skinhead grinned as he took off the backpack and placed it on the leather booth. "I move around. Originally from Bakersfield, California."

"Long way from home," O'Keefe said.

"It's a fucking toilet here on the East Coast. I work job to job, you know how it is. Wherever the work is."

O'Keefe nodded.

"Yeah, New York, not my kind of place."

"It has its moments."

The kid made small talk for a few minutes, then said, "Crazy shit going down today."

O'Keefe took a couple gulps of the beer, quenching his thirst. "Yeah, so I heard. What can I tell you? Shit happens, right?"

"Don't like cops. Well, they don't seem to like me."

"You run into any trouble here in the city?"

"Not so far. But I can handle myself, don't worry about that."

"Son, you got something for me?"

The skinhead smiled. "Thought you'd never ask." He pushed the backpack under the table. "I was told to give you that."

O'Keefe lifted it up and placed it beside him in the booth. "What's in it?"

"Some parts you might need. And some cash. A nice new ID, car keys, and a credit card. A friend of mine specializes in IDs and whatever you want. That's why they brought me in for this."

"Good work."

The skinhead drank the rest of his beer and stood up. "One final thing. Three blocks from here, parking garage, second floor, cab is waiting. Take care, man."

Then the kid turned and walked out.

O'Keefe drank the rest of his beer. He waited a few minutes. He picked up the backpack and headed to the restroom, checking there was no one in it. He took the end stall and locked the door. He sent an encrypted message that read *Bakersfield, California.*

A short while later, a reply with a telephone number pinged up.

O'Keefe called the number. On the other end of the line, a familiar gruff voice. It was the shot caller. Thomas "Mad Dog" Mills.

"You still on for tonight?" Mills asked.

"What do you think?"

"You get the delivery?"

"Yeah, smart kid. Just about to head out and catch the ride."

"The guy's waiting for you. I'm hearing you really fucked up those cops downtown, man."

O'Keefe felt a mixture of pride and elation hearing it from Mills. He only wished his brothers were alive to savor the moment. He knew what they'd do if they were. They'd hug him tight as if he were still the skinny youngest brother they had to defend. Then buy him a beer and tousle his hair. He always enjoyed listening to his older brothers. He wasn't a big talker. But by God, they were. Never stopped. "Tell me, the attorney general, did we get him?"

"That is a negative."

"What happened?"

"I'm hearing from a ham radio friend that he got the narc."

"That's something."

"But when Charlie's brother got to the AG's house, the fucker wasn't in. Apparently, Bobby got blown away by some Fed."

"How the hell did they get there?"

"I don't know."

"So where is the AG?"

A beat. "Why do you want to know, Todd? That wasn't your target."

"I know. But I'd like to know where he is."

"I know what you're thinking, man. I can almost hear the cogs in that brain of yours grinding around."

"Where is he?"

"You're a crazy son of a bitch, Todd."

"So do you know where the fucker is or not?"

The shot caller sighed. "I do."

"I want to know."

"That might be one too many diversions. Shouldn't we focus on the next stage?"

"Just tell me."

"I'm hearing from two separate sources that he's holed up in his new Midtown office, three blocks from Penn Station."

"That's interesting."

"Not too far from your final destination."

O'Keefe was weighing the options.

"I know what you're thinking, man. But my concern is that you won't have enough time."

"There's always enough time. I'm going back into the city anyway."

"Stay safe, bro. And I'll keep you posted on any developments."

Twenty-Four

A bloodred sunset washed over the Manhattan sky, reflecting off the glass towers, as Reznick's chopper landed at the Midtown heliport. He thought of Lauren out on the streets with her friends, unaware of Todd O'Keefe and the threat he posed to the city. He prayed to God she would be safe. But he was comforted by the fact that Lauren had shown a steely determination earlier that day, after the sniper attack outside Yankee Stadium. She hadn't panicked. She hadn't started screaming. She was stoic. She reminded Reznick so much of her mother. He wondered if his preconceived notions of what kind of person Lauren was were off the mark. The quiet girl. The studious girl. Maybe she was a lot more like him than he cared to admit.

A waiting medical examiner loaded Greer's body onto a gurney and into the back of an ambulance.

Reznick touched the back of Greer's cold hand, then climbed into a waiting FBI Lincoln. Waves of exhaustion washed over him as the exertions of the day finally hit. It seemed to seep down into his very bones. He did what he always did. He popped a Dexedrine with some water. He needed to stay in the fight.

A few minutes later, he was back downtown at the FBI's New York City field office. It was only a mile from where the two female cops had been mown down in the Financial District.

Reznick rode the elevator with a couple of Feds for company. He began to feel the drug kick in. He felt more wired. Switched on. The way he liked it. The way he had to be.

"You need to get some rest, Jon," one of the Feds said. "Brutal day you've had."

Reznick sipped from a bottle of water. "I'll survive."

"Do you need to see a doctor at all?"

"Probably a psychiatrist, but no, thanks for asking."

The Fed gave a rueful smile. "I heard what happened out in Long Island. You just seem to attract trouble."

"Ain't that the truth."

The Fed patted him on the back. "I for one am glad you're on our side. And glad you're safe."

"Appreciate that."

His colleague just nodded and smiled but didn't speak.

Reznick was escorted to a restroom, where he cleaned up. He was then shown into a conference room where Meyerstein was waiting, coffee in hand, standing in front of a huge screen. It displayed a grainy black-and-white photograph of a tattooed Aryan Brotherhood guy. "Shut the door behind you," she said.

Reznick slumped in a seat, the Dexedrine rousing his system.

"You look beat," she said. She poured a black coffee for Reznick and placed it in front of him along with some sandwiches. "Hopefully this will revitalize you."

Reznick smiled. "You do this for all your special agents?"

"Only the ones who worry the hell out of me, night and day."

Reznick shrugged. "What can I tell you?" The strong scalding coffee was welcome. Then he wolfed down a couple of ham sandwiches.

Meyerstein handed him a napkin. "Want some more?"

Reznick shook his head as he wiped the crumbs from his mouth.

"Feel better?"

"Marginally. Thanks."

Reznick took another gulp of the hot coffee. The caffeine jolt felt good. "I don't know about you, but I'm struggling to get my head around what's really going on. There are so many components. So many moving parts. We're just scratching the surface. I mean, what the hell is going on here, Martha?"

"We're focused on the information Cortez has passed on, deliberately or inadvertently. He's going to be interviewed. OPR is picking him up in half an hour."

"Where is he?"

"Having a cup of coffee, strung out. And he's remorseful."

"Well, that's just great."

"Our top priority is finding Todd O'Keefe."

"I want to talk about this agent for a moment. What the hell went wrong?"

"Drug habit, apparently. Started off innocuously on pain medication. Had some fall while out on a job. He was a fine special agent, by all accounts. But the addiction to the painkillers took hold. Oxycodone. Then heroin. Then he took methadone to cope after he came off the heroin. And also managed to function by popping Percocet, another opioid, to get through the day."

"Seriously?"

Meyerstein nodded. "Awful, I know. But there's also a woman in his life. A fiancée."

"Well, that sounds like a lovely twenty-first-century love story in the making."

"So we're looking into her too."

Reznick gulped some of his coffee. "Let's get back to what we know happened today. So, we've got eight cops dead, killed by the two O'Keefe brothers, who are now dead. A dead ex-cop, Jimmy Greer, killed by Charlie Campbell's brother, who is now dead. Two more dead cops, killed by Todd O'Keefe, who is still on the loose. Am I missing something? This isn't the kind of operation that was put together over a few beers at a bar. It couldn't have been. This took serious planning."

Meyerstein began to pace the room, gazing out over the early-evening downtown skyline. "I know."

Reznick leaned back in the seat. "Did you learn anything more from Cortez?"

"Mostly what I told you on the phone. He's a functioning addict. And according to Cortez, he was being blackmailed by some guys who had photos of him taking drugs. They gave him an endless supply of heroin, and in return he 'lost' Robert O'Keefe's note, but we also believe he persuaded a supervisory agent here in New York not to pursue the surveillance of the O'Keefes the FBI was actively involved with."

"It doesn't just come down to one fucked-up special agent, though, surely."

"You're talking about Campbell's contacts and connections?"

"Precisely. Greer mentioned the DEA and CIA."

"I've put together a team at HQ to examine this. It's serious. We'll get to the bottom of this."

"Martha, the FBI needs to be absolutely clear that this compromised agent was just the tip of the iceberg. It would be the easiest thing in the world to lay the blame solely on Cortez. Bottom line? I'm not buying that Cortez had inside knowledge on Greer, where he lived, and on the attorney general. You would need inside knowledge. I think that's above his pay grade. And he's just a fucking cog."

"So what do you think?"

"US intelligence agencies, maybe CIA."

Meyerstein's gaze wandered around the room as if she were deep in thought. "You have no proof of that."

"No, I don't. That's your responsibility."

"We'll get to the bottom of this, mark my words."

Reznick shook his head. "You know how it works. The blame is going to be put on Cortez. It's the way it is. You need a fall guy. But a cursory look at what we know tells me that this doesn't start and end with Cortez. True, he might have passed along classified information. But for the DOJ to get involved, and for Greer to get retired from the force for asking questions, means this all goes higher up. Someone wanted to shut down any investigation into Campbell, the link to drugs being run by the Brotherhood and MS-13, and the full extent of the O'Keefes' involvement."

Meyerstein stared at him, stony faced.

"Is that a fair assessment?"

"It's a damning assessment, Jon, I'll give you that."

"It's the truth."

"No one really knows, Jon."

"Do you think you'll find out?"

Meyerstein shrugged. "Intelligence gathering is sometimes all smoke and mirrors. But I believe your assessment has merit. I'll be mentioning it to my team."

Reznick nodded.

Meyerstein crossed her arms as she paced the room. She turned around, stopped, hands resting on the back of a chair opposite Reznick, staring him down. "You should know that our computer forensic examiners have accessed Cortez's work and personal laptops. There are signs that he's been passing sensitive, highly classified information about investigations, including into the O'Keefes, on to third parties."

Reznick stared at her.

"We believe that some classified details were sent through a highly encrypted messaging system to a former college friend of his. DEA."

"Martha, that's an outrageous breach."

Meyerstein sighed. "The investigation is still ongoing, but Cortez insists his fiancée is innocent. He's talking freely, but we're concerned for her safety."

"So where is she?"

"That's the thing. We don't know. We've tried tracking her via her cell phone, but nothing. The problem for us is that she appears to be clean. Excellent employment record. But our analysts did find something."

"What's that?"

Meyerstein jabbed the remote at the huge screen and pressed a button. Up on the screen was a grainy color photo of two Hispanic guys, heavily tattooed. "We've also trawled the surveillance footage in and around Cortez's apartment in Gowanus. These two charmers were caught on camera outside the agent's apartment building on three separate occasions within the last month."

"I'm guessing they're not neighborhood watch."

"Both are members of MS-13. And I don't believe there are a lot of them in this part of Brooklyn. We've also just discovered that the fiancée's parents are Mexican. And we are surmising that MS-13 have identified the girl, and approached her too, threatening her with violence to either her or her parents back in Mexico, unless she does them a favor. So they've got Cortez with photos using drugs, and they might have a hold over her too, with threats against her family."

"That would keep a lot of people in check."

"She might be part of MS-13, but I'm not buying it. I think she's being targeted. That's what my instincts are telling me, as well as the facts and her track record." Meyerstein pressed another button on the remote, and a beaming picture of a pretty Latina girl appeared on the screen. "No tattoos. No markings. She's a hardworking customs officer at JFK. Quite religious."

"JFK, huh? Which would be very useful to MS-13, with regards to smuggling, whether it's people, drugs, you name it."

"That occurred to us too."

Reznick gulped down the rest of his coffee. "This day just gets crazier."

"We need to find her. And quick."

"First we need to find Todd O'Keefe." Reznick looked out the window as the sky turned crimson. "July fourth. Fucking crazy, crazy day."

Meyerstein sighed. "I meant to tell you, we tried to contact Lauren, but we couldn't get through. We can't trace her location."

"I wonder if her phone died."

"That was about an hour and a half ago."

Reznick took out his cell phone and called his daughter. It rang six times before she finally answered.

"Hey, Dad," Lauren said breezily, as if she didn't have a care in the world.

Reznick gave a sigh of relief. "Thank God, honey. Where have you been? I've been trying to call you. So have the FBI."

"Ran out of juice after being out so late last night. No charger . . . But it's fixed now." The signal began to cut out. "I borrowed a charger from a friend."

"Where are you now?"

"I'm with my friends, Dad."

Reznick sat up in his seat. "Have you seen the news?"

"Yes, I have, Dad. I know. It's terrible."

"This is a serious ongoing situation. I'm concerned that you're out there on the streets while this is all going on. This is dangerous. You're not taking it seriously."

"This is New York, Dad. I love the city. I'm surrounded by millions of people. I'm not going anywhere. Do you think these nutcases who carried out the attacks are going to change me? Scare me? Not a chance. To hell with them."

Suddenly, a female agent burst into the room. "Ma'am, quick, it's Cortez."

Reznick ended the call, brushed past Meyerstein, and followed the agent down a corridor to the restroom. Two officers were trying to kick down the locked door. "What the hell's going on?"

"Cortez isn't answering. He locked it from the inside."

Reznick said, "Step back!"

The two Feds moved aside.

Reznick pulled out his Beretta and fired two shots into the lock. It split apart and he kicked open the door. He rushed inside. But it was too late.

Lying sprawled at the far stall, door open, was Cortez. Eyes shut, white powder and blood around his nose.

Reznick rushed over and kneeled down. He pulled back Cortez's eyelids. No pupil dilation. He turned around and looked up at the Feds in the doorway. "You got a medical kit? We need Narcan! And call the paramedics!"

One of the Feds nodded and disappeared.

Reznick slapped Cortez's clammy face. "Wake up, Leon! You need to wake up!"

A few moments later, the Fed returned with a medical backpack. He unzipped it and handed a Narcan nasal spray to Reznick.

Reznick ripped off the packaging and removed the device. He inserted the nozzle into Cortez's right nostril and firmly pressed the plunger, releasing the anti-opioid drugs into the nose. He checked his watch. "Still no sign of life. We need to bring him back quick!"

The Fed kneeled beside him and took out a bag-valve mask. The manual resuscitator was placed carefully over Cortez's mouth and nose.

Reznick began to massage Cortez's chest. "Come on, man, wake the fuck up! You can do this. But you gotta wake up."

The Fed took off the mask. "No response. Another dose?"

Reznick nodded and inserted the Narcan nozzle into the left nostril and again pressed the plunger. "Come on, Leon, snap out of it!"

The mask was again placed over Cortez's mouth and nose as they desperately tried to revive the special agent.

Reznick checked his watch. A full three minutes had gone. The seconds were ticking by. He clapped his hands in front of Cortez's face.

"Wake up, Leon! Snap out of it, man!" He saw a flicker in the eyelids. He looked at the Fed beside him. "Remove the mask."

"What?"

"Just do it!"

The Fed took the mask off Cortez's face.

Reznick cradled Cortez's head and leaned in close. "Wake up, man! Wake up! Come on, man, just wake the fuck up! I know you're in there." His tone became sharper. "Come on, son, time to wake up!"

Suddenly, Cortez opened his eyes wide, gasping for air.

Twenty-Five

Perez felt in a happier frame of mind after speaking to Leon. She walked toward his tiny apartment in Gowanus, just off Ninth Street, overlooking the canal. The drink had taken the edge off her nerves. She sidestepped a pile of vomit and dog shit on the sidewalk. It wasn't the nicest part of Brooklyn, that was for sure. But as far as she was concerned, it was a hell of a lot better than Hempstead.

She liked the bohemian vibe. And no one knew her here. That was an attraction. She liked the cool bars. The buzz. It was fantastically close to Manhattan. But it was also perfect for accessing the nice restaurants in upscale Park Slope, and the delightful Prospect Park.

She loved nothing better than walking in Prospect Park with Leon, usually on a Sunday, which fit in with their work schedules. She wondered if they would ever be in a position to buy their own home. Maybe not in Park Slope, because that was just crazy. But maybe somewhere nearby. Gowanus would be fine. She hoped they could get a nice place, perhaps with room for her mother and father. She missed her mother's company very much. She envisioned looking after her parents more and more. She knew they would help her get Leon back on the straight and narrow.

Perhaps more than anything, she daydreamed of having kids, moving to Brooklyn with Leon, even if they only rented. She imagined herself pushing a stroller, not having to worry about lowlifes, gangs, and God knew what in Hempstead, and enjoying what the city had to offer.

The more she thought about it, the more she wanted a few children. Four. Why not? She loved kids. Eventually, Leon would earn a promotion at the FBI. He could get his master's degree. Study nights. She had also thought of going to college and majoring in international business. A friend from her high school days had started at Hofstra University in Hempstead and was loving it. Perez had watched the way her friend seemed to blossom. She talked about books, business, the internet, deals, Bloomberg, on and on. She seemed like she suddenly had a career to look forward to, as opposed to a job.

Perez longed to put the bullshit lines she had to contend with at JFK behind her. Having to check surly passengers and their families. Some could speak only Spanish and accused her of discriminating against people from Guatemala, Mexico, El Salvador, or wherever they were flying in from. She invariably tried to explain, in perfect Spanish, that her parents were from Mexico, and she didn't discriminate against anyone, but only wanted to stop visitors whose visas were not in order, or who might be in possession of drugs or other contraband. But they continued to regard her with suspicion. It was draining. Depressing. It ground her down.

Perez didn't want that life anymore. She wanted a family life. Stability. In recent months, she and Leon had talked about her moving in. She had a key to his apartment. And that was when she discovered, for the first time, the shocking fact that Leon was a functioning opiate addict. She was devastated. She had been helping him kick his habit since then. He had taken methadone for a while. It seemed to settle him down. She had put him in touch with drug therapy units. But only two weeks earlier, she had seen the burnt aluminum foil in the trash in his apartment's tiny galley-style kitchen. He was back on the junk.

Perez wanted to believe in him. She wanted to believe it was an aberration. But the reality was staring her in the face: Leon was chasing the dragon again. He said it was only oxycodone to ease his pain. But the new marks on his arm told another story. Whatever it was, she knew he still couldn't shake it. She had tried to get him to see an addiction counselor. Maybe even a psychologist to talk through his problems. But to no avail. He was terrified that it would get out, and his secret would be revealed to his bosses at the FBI.

What amazed her most was that he was still able to function. Usually he took a Percocet and he would get through the day, all smiles. Then when he came home, exhausted, he would do a bit of junk, invariably laced with fentanyl. She sometimes wondered how his bosses didn't notice. But Leon was very good at masking both his feelings and any minor ailments.

She had tried to nurse him through withdrawal a couple of months earlier during a one-week vacation. She'd watched over him, making sure he wasn't taking anything. She fed him soup, vitamins, and water. But Leon's cold turkey was bad. He sweated, crawled the walls, like he had the worst flu in the world. He was like a caged animal. Somehow, despite the drug cravings, in that week he got off the opiates. No drugs. Zero. But the next time she saw him, she could tell he was back on it. His eyes were sunken, red, tired, glazed.

Perez wondered if it was worth it, trying to change her addict fiancé. Her friends had told her that she was crazy and that he had to get clean before she should consider marrying him. But she persevered. She loved him. And she thought he loved her too.

Perez was afraid. Leon's addiction was turning criminal. He just shrugged it off. With a nonchalance, maybe arrogance, she didn't like to see in him. A side of him she hadn't seen before.

She often wondered if she shouldn't have just cut and run. Her father had been an alcoholic as a young man, and her mother, virtually a saint in his eyes, had nursed him until he became sober. Clean and healthy from his thirtieth birthday onward. Perez was no saint. She didn't want to be a saint, a Mother Teresa, or anything like that. But something within her, something deep within the very fiber of her being, would not let her abandon her fiancé. Just like her mother had with her father, she felt as if she could save Leon.

Perez believed Leon's intimate knowledge of the gangs, informers, dealers, and enforcers had gotten him too easily embroiled in their world. The painkillers had led to addiction, which led to him knowing exactly which gangbangers to go to for more drugs. The very people he'd spent his career trying to stop now had a hold over him. The fact that now they had decided to make contact with her too was very worrying. She thought it was just a matter of time before they asked her to usher their drug mules through her line at JFK.

She felt trapped. In a bind. But how to escape?

A car alarm in the distance snapped Perez out of her daydream. She was close to Leon's apartment.

Something—maybe a prickle at the back of her neck—made her sense she was being watched. She turned around. In the distance, the pickup truck came into view. Inside were the same two gangbangers. They had tailed her to Gowanus. But how? She had taken the train. Were they tracking her cell phone? Or was it only coincidence that they'd ended up near Leon's apartment at the same time she arrived?

Her stomach tightened. She kept on walking, unsure what to do. *Think, for God's sake.*

Perez's mind raced. It felt wrong. Everything felt wrong. She sensed they were no longer here just to warn her. But what the hell did they want?

Were they fucking with her? Did they want her to pass on a message to Leon?

149

She wondered if she should just stop in the middle of the sidewalk, turn around, and walk right up to them. Perhaps confront them. Make a scene in front of passersby. Start screaming, *Rape!*

But guys like that wouldn't be fazed if bystanders got involved. They'd just shoot the innocents or pistol-whip them. They didn't care. What about if she ran into a bar? A restaurant? But she pictured them heading inside, dragging her out, and killing her or anyone that resisted.

Something was seriously wrong.

Her stomach began to cramp. Panic setting in.

Oh my God, I can't bear this!

Were they just waiting to pounce?

Leon's apartment was only three hundred, maybe four hundred, yards away. She realized she wouldn't get there in time. But if they were going to harm her, why not do it right now, with her in their sights? What the hell was going on? Were they waiting until she was at the apartment? Away from the main traffic in Gowanus?

The more she thought about what to do, the more conflicted she became. She was faced with a simple, terrible dilemma. Fight or flight? But what about the consequences for her family back in Mexico? She knew MS-13 had links to that part of the world as well as El Salvador, where the founding members had come from. To other gangs. Organizations. Hempstead was full of guys like that. She also knew they would have insiders, maybe baggage handlers, who worked at JFK. Maybe some that had access to her records? Her parents' home? What about them?

Perez pulled out her cell phone and decided she had to call Leon. She thought she was going to pass out from the tension. She could almost feel the men's eyes on her. His phone rang once.

A woman's voice at the other end of the line said, "Camila Perez?"

Perez wondered who was using Leon's cell phone. She assumed it had to be a coworker. "I'm sorry, who's this?"

"Camila, this is FBI assistant director Martha Meyerstein."

"I—I'm sorry . . . I'm looking to speak to my fiancé, Leon. It's urgent."

"Listen to me, Camila. Leon is in trouble. Deep trouble. And we need to speak to you urgently."

Perez's heart sank. "What?"

"Camila, you need to pay attention. Leon is not OK. We've got a serious situation here."

Perez wondered if they'd found out about his addiction. "Is he sick? Is he OK?"

"Leon is fighting for his life. He is receiving medical attention. But he is under arrest. Do you understand?"

Perez felt herself go into what felt like shock.

"Camila, are you still there?"

"Yes, I'm still here."

"We need to talk. And I mean right now. This is a grave situation. But you probably realize that already."

The news crashed through her head like a ten-ton truck. She felt as if she were having an out-of-body experience. "I'm sorry, I don't understand."

"You will soon. Where are you?"

"I'm in Brooklyn."

"We've been trying to find you."

"I'd like to speak to Leon first."

"You will. But we need to speak to you. Face-to-face. I'm concerned for your safety."

Perez turned and saw that the pickup had pulled up at the side of the road. She wondered whether to trust the woman claiming to be a Fed on the other end of the line. "I don't know who you are. How do I know you're from the FBI?"

"Camila, I'm assuming you know that Leon has been leading a double life. We believe he's been compromised. Seriously compromised.

I saw the track marks on his arms. We didn't have any idea. No one in the New York field office did. But he's in over his head. He told me everything."

Perez closed her eyes, wanting to burst out crying.

"He took an overdose. I think we got to him in time. What else do you want to know?"

Perez said, "Is he going to live?"

"He's conscious. He's in the hospital."

"I need to see him."

"You will. Where are you? We can't get a fix on your cell phone."

"Leon advised me to get a VPN. Apparently it masks location." Which meant that wasn't how the guys in the pickup had found her.

"Switch it off, Camila. We need to know where you are."

Perez did as she was told. "OK, turned it off."

"Alright, just a second . . ." A few moments later, Meyerstein said, "OK, we got a precise fix. I've got some people en route. Federal agents. They'll get you here safely."

"I'm scared."

"Look, we'll figure it all out. We need to know what damage has been done."

"I'm scared about what's going to happen to Leon. He's not a bad person. I don't want him to go to jail."

"I can't make any promises. But he needs to cooperate to stand a chance."

"He will. He just needs help. A lot of help."

"And he'll get it. We'll get him professional help. To be honest, the fact that the New York field office was oblivious to his problem is negligent on their part. So it's not just Leon with problems, let me tell you."

Perez felt tears in her eyes. "I've got my own problem. A real problem. Right now."

"What kind of problem?"

"I'm so scared."

"No reason to be scared. We'll figure it out."

"You don't understand. Please listen to me, I think I'm in danger. There are two men following me. I think they're MS-13."

"Do you mean they're following you right now?"

"Correct. They called me earlier. They seemed to be watching me this afternoon when I was on Long Island."

"What's the license plate?"

Perez had memorized it and gave the details. "I think they're in a gang. Gang tattoos. And I'm worried they might kill me or my family in Mexico. I think these are the guys Leon might be involved with. Getting drugs from. They're blackmailing him."

"Camila, we've got a fix on your location, and I can see you're nearly at Leon's apartment. Gowanus. Eleventh Street. Get yourself inside."

Perez felt herself beginning to panic the closer she got. "I'm scared. I don't think I'll make it in time. They pulled over. And now they're just watching me."

"Stay calm."

"But I'm not calm. I'm frightened."

"Listen to me, can you get into a bar or restaurant where there are people?"

"You don't know what these guys are like. They're crazy. MS-13, I think."

"OK . . . Are you listening?"

"Yeah, I'm listening."

"Camila, we know where you are. But you need to get away from those guys. Fast. We don't know how they'll react."

"So what the hell should I do?!"

"Try not to panic. Find a place where you can stay out of sight. But you need to move."

Perez ended the call and turned away from the guys in the car. She pressed the cell phone to her ear, as if taking a routine call. Her heart was pounding like a pneumatic drill. She was wearing comfortable sneakers. Thankfully no heels. She felt a surge of adrenaline. She was scared witless.

Do it, Camila! Do it now!

She took off and ran. Sprinted headlong down the busy street. Turned onto a sketchy road lined with industrial shops and garages. Down a lane and across the street and into a bar. Past the shocked drinkers. "There are two guys chasing me!" she yelled.

The drinkers just stared at her as she ran through the back. Then through the kitchen, bumping into a cook.

"Hey, what the fuck, lady?"

Perez barged out of a back door and down a dark side street.

A couple of girls were smoking cigarettes.

"What's the matter, hon?" one girl said.

Perez ran past her as if possessed. Her heart felt like it was going to burst. She was gasping for air as she sprinted past the canal. The pale moon reflected on the dark water. She ran across a bridge and down another street, praying she had given them the slip.

A quick glance back showed the truck was on her tail. Just over 150 yards or so behind her. And closing. She wasn't going to outrun them. She needed to hide.

Perez ran across the road in front of a car. The vehicle had to brake hard to avoid her. She continued, heart rate nearly at the max. Adrenaline was rushing through her body. She felt as if every sense were switched on. Down a dark road. She felt frantic. She was being hunted. Like an animal.

A hipster girl had her hands in the air as if in submission. "Slow down, girl, what's wrong?"

"Call the police!"

The girl stared at her as if she'd lost her mind.

Perez tore down the street, past industrial buildings, and through an open space. She ran toward a warehouse cloaked in darkness. She felt a sense of dread. Gnawing at her guts. She felt sick. Where was she running to? Why was she running? And it dawned on her. Had she made the wrong choice? Maybe she should have hidden in the bar. With other people. Stayed with the crowds. Maybe they could have protected her. But she didn't want to endanger innocent people. She knew the guys who were chasing her. They were crazy. They would shoot up a place if they needed to. Killing was no big deal to them. Oh God, what was she going to do? Where were the cops? Where was Leon? Where was she? She was lost. All alone. God, no!

A cyclist cut across her path and screamed, "You fucking idiot, look where you're going!"

Perez kicked down a wooden fence and ran behind the building. She bounded up some stairs connected to a loading bay. She barged through a door, already hanging off its hinges. She banged into some pallets as she ran through a huge dark, cavernous space. The smell of piss and excrement. Graffitied walls. She wanted to gag. But she kept running.

She ran to the far side of the warehouse. She barged through a door. Then up more stairs. Two at a time. And along a windowless corridor.

Perez felt she was spiraling into a nightmare in the long-forgotten canal-front warehouse. She pushed on through double swing doors on an upper floor. She didn't want to die in such a place. In such circumstances. She wasn't going to let them kill her. She was going to fight to stay alive.

She was panting hard as she ran down corridor after corridor. She needed to focus. She needed to think. She needed a place to hide. *Think!* She would hide until the FBI could find her. But how long would that be? She had to trust that they were on their way and would get to her.

She crunched through broken glass and slipped, feeling a sharp jab in her hand. She was bleeding, but there was no time to do anything about it. She headed down another corridor, guessing that she was in the office space of an old factory or storage depot.

Think, damn it, think!

Perez stopped for a second. She froze. Somewhere down below, maybe on the ground floor, footsteps echoed on the concrete floors. They were closing in. They had her trapped.

She climbed up more stairs. She prayed they couldn't see the trail of blood in the dark space. But occasionally chinks of light from broken windows allowed some moonlight to seep in, bathing the interior with an ethereal glow.

The place was freaking her out. The guys following her were freaking her out.

She didn't know whether to climb higher or try to slip out without them catching her. Perhaps down separate stairs. Should she just jump out of a fucking window and be done with it? Should she try and get up onto the roof? Perhaps lock it so they couldn't get up. But the chances were that once it was opened, that was that. They could get up too.

Perez racked her brains. Her mind was frozen in fear. Unable to process her thoughts. She wanted to arm herself. But with what?

Move!

She swiveled her head. Watching, listening. Her eyes were becoming more accustomed to the darkness. She saw a door down the corridor.

Perez took a deep breath. And she bolted down the corridor. Through the heavy wooden door and up more stairs. Through another set of doors and along a creaking corridor.

Suddenly, her right foot plunged through a rotten floorboard, a rusty nail ripping through her skin.

Perez felt an eruption of shooting pain in her leg. She clenched her teeth, sucking up the pain, tears spilling down her face. She would not cry out. Slowly she extricated herself from the rotten floorboard and got up. She headed into a huge cavernous concrete space again. She wasn't going to go down without a fight.

At the far end of the space, she could make out a plasterboard wall. It looked like part of it had been ripped out, maybe by squatters. She squeezed behind it, back to the brick wall. It was a tight, dusty space. She edged sideways, like a crab, deeper behind the plasterboard. Eventually, she squeezed past a concrete pillar, then crouched down behind it, tasting salty tears, bleeding onto the dusty brick floor. As a hiding spot, this was the best she could do.

The sound of her rapid breathing was all she heard.

Perez closed her eyes. She wanted to cry. For Leon to turn up and hold her. Tell her he was going to get clean. And it was all going to be OK. He wasn't going to go to jail. But she needed to stay strong. She needed to hang in there. Tough it out. Her mother was tough. Perez would just have to be resilient, like her. She needed to find that inner strength.

She tried to reassure herself. The Feds were on their way. That was good. It was just a matter of minutes; hopefully she could hang on.

Perez's breathing became shallower. The only sound was of her beating heart. Time seemed to have stopped. Seconds were lifetimes. So many lifetimes.

Her mind flashed back to when she was a child. She could see herself playing hide-and-seek with her friends. Hiding in a loft space of an abandoned building. She remembered the mixture of tension and fear, knowing she might be discovered at any moment.

A droplet of blood seeped from her leg onto the stone floor. She wondered where the men were. Were they closing in? Then again, maybe they would miss her?

Suddenly, she heard them.

The sound of scuffed footsteps. Low voices. Maybe just outside in the corridor. She heard a door squeak open. Creaking wooden floorboards. It was them. She couldn't believe they had found her.

Perez closed her eyes tighter, sensed them close. Looking around. Trying to detect any movement or noise. Hunting their prey.

"She's not far," one Hispanic voice said.

The other said, "Yeah, the bitch is here. I can smell her. Real close."

"We know you're here, bitch. I can almost taste you. We'll find you. You're in here somewhere. And we've got all the time in the world. What the fuck you thinking about? Running away like that? We just wanted to talk to you. We wouldn't hurt you."

Perez felt herself shaking. She shut her eyes tight and began to pray.

Twenty-Six

The convoy of SUVs was speeding through the streets of Gowanus, Brooklyn, closing in on Camila Perez's location. Reznick was sitting up front in the lead vehicle, three other Feds in the back. More Feds in the two following cars. Reznick checked his iPhone, which showed Camila's precise location, a warehouse.

The driver said, "One mile."

Reznick turned to the Feds in the back seat. "Block off this road. If the cops or anyone asks on whose authority, this comes from FBI HQ."

A surly-looking Fed said, "We don't report to you, Jon."

"I'm not asking you to report to me. I'm asking you guys to make sure we don't turn this into a social media circus, news crews turning up."

The guy averted his gaze. He was clearly not happy having Reznick with them.

Reznick looked at the rest of the agents. "Just so we're clear. I'm not giving orders. But I've been given specific instructions by Assistant Director Meyerstein. She wants me in first. You got a problem, you speak to her. Which one of you guys wants to volunteer to get their head blown off by being the first in?"

A deafening silence.

"So, I'm leading on this. You got a problem, speak to her."

The Fed said nothing but was clearly seething that the usual rules of engagement and protocol weren't being observed.

"My advice?" Reznick said. "Send in two teams of three through separate entrances in two minutes. I'll get in first and see if I can find these bastards. I'll report if I get a visual."

The Fed said, "I've never met you. I had no idea that we operated like this. I think we need to establish clear authority."

"You need to pay attention. Assistant Director Meyerstein gave me authority. Take it up with her."

The Fed said, "This little outing is going to follow FBI standard operating procedure."

"You need to get out more, pal."

"Fuck you, I'm going in with you. We all are."

Reznick stared at the intransigent Fed. "Listen, we can discuss all this bullshit until the cows come home. My orders come from the top. I go in first. I just want a minute's head start to see if I can locate them. Get a visual. SWAT is on their way. Just keep the perimeter in place. And make sure they don't slip through the dragnet."

"This is irregular."

"Not half as irregular as your colleague Leon Cortez." Reznick didn't mention that Cortez had overdosed; the news was being kept under wraps while they investigated his connections. "You wanna talk about that?"

The guy just sat and stared, lost for words.

"You wanna talk about how he compromised FBI activities?" Reznick looked at the other agents, who just stared blankly back at him. "No? Thought not."

Reznick was livid as they turned onto a narrow road leading toward the warehouse. He was used to being part of a tight-knit Delta crew who took orders, gave orders, and operated as a team. He couldn't handle pettiness. He wanted to get the job done. And then get out of there.

In the distance he saw the vehicle Perez had identified as following her. "This looks like it," he said.

The SUV pulled up, and Reznick turned around to face the Feds in the back seat. "I'm going in there. You gonna cover me?"

They all nodded. "You got it," the youngest Fed said. "This is just outside our usual methods."

"We want the same thing. We want that young woman in the warehouse found safe. Right?"

More nods.

"Good. Let's get to it."

Reznick got out of the vehicle and quickly headed down a path adjacent to the canal as the Feds from the back seat fanned out, setting up the cordon. He jogged down the path for a couple hundred yards. He crunched over some broken glass. He wanted to approach the warehouse out of sight. The streetlights beside the building were getting brighter.

He reached up and pulled himself to the top of the brick wall, peering over the other side. No sign of the gangbangers. He clambered over and lowered himself down.

Reznick felt his heart rate begin to rise. He moved toward the loading dock of the abandoned warehouse. He bounded up the steps and pulled open the door.

He allowed the streetlights to bathe some of the dark space. Then he spotted a door diagonally across. He wedged open the door with half a brick.

"Northwest door on the canal side open," he whispered via his headset to the Feds who would be following him in. "Proceed with caution."

Reznick moved quietly across the floor. He pushed open a door that led to a stairwell. He bounded up two flights of stairs and crouched down. He heard voices. Farther up. He moved to the next level. He ran up one more flight and through a door.

Gun drawn, he headed down a long corridor.

A few yards in front of him, something glistened on the wooden floor. He edged forward and crouched down, trying to get his bearings.

Reznick touched the substance. It was warm blood, congealing. He saw another spot of blood a yard away. He wondered if Camila Perez had injured herself fleeing for her life. He moved along the narrow space gingerly, testing the rotten floorboards and trying not to make them creak.

His senses were switched on.

Reznick stopped. He listened for any sounds. He detected voices, talking low, in Spanish. Then the sound of footsteps way down below on the ground level. The sound of a handgun slide being racked. Those had to be the other Feds, perhaps the SWAT backup who'd been on their way.

A guy cleared his throat on the other side of the door. "Hey, Camila," he said in English. "I know you're in here." It was the mocking voice of one of the gangbangers. "You're gonna come out, you little bitch. No one runs from us."

Reznick lay down on his stomach and leaned forward. He cracked the door with his handgun. Two spectral figures prowled through the darkened space. One was wearing a white T-shirt, the other a slightly luminous lime-green top, easy to see in the darkness.

"I know you're in here," the voice said. "I don't know why you're scared."

Reznick sensed they had her cornered in the room.

Down below, maybe directly underneath, heavy footsteps. Movement. The Feds were closing in.

Reznick eased the door open a couple of inches. The man in the green top made a signal to the second guy. He swiped his hand in a curved motion, indicating that the girl was hiding behind what looked like a partition wall.

The guy in the white T-shirt nodded, crouched down, and turned on his cell phone light. "I see some blood." The thug moved closer and stared behind the portioned wall. "Ah, there you are, you little bitch! Come out!"

Reznick aimed at the guy in the white T-shirt. He fired two shots to his head. The thug collapsed to the ground. The deafening noise echoed around the brick walls and dark space.

The guy in green spun around.

Reznick didn't wait. He fired two more shots into the center of the guy's chest. The guy collapsed in a heap, moaning and writhing on the ground as his gun dropped to the stone floor.

Reznick got up, barged through the door, gun trained on the moaning thug. The sound of weeping came from behind the partition wall.

Reznick approached the prostrate gangbanger and kicked the thug's gun out of reach.

"What the fuck, man!" the guy wailed. "Please, I ain't got no problem with you, man."

Reznick stood over the thug, gun trained on his head.

"Please, don't kill me!" the guy screamed. "I surrender, man. You win."

Reznick stared down at him and smiled. "You don't seem so tough now, Mr. MS-13. You like intimidating innocent people? You like threatening a nice young lady? That make you feel tough? Does it?"

"No, man, it's all just a crazy misunderstanding."

"A crazy misunderstanding, is that right?"

"I swear. It was mistaken identity. We thought this woman threatened my family. I love my family."

"You really are a lying piece of shit, aren't you? Do you think anyone will miss you when you're gone?"

The guy gritted his teeth as if in acute pain. "I fucked up, I know. I fucked up. I'll face the consequences."

Reznick pointed the handgun at his head. "You're damn right you will."

Tears filled the guy's eyes. "Man, slow down, what are you doing? Are you crazy? I'm not armed now! I am not armed! What the hell do you think you're doing?"

"You're going away for a long, long time, maggot."

The guy began to grin. "Maybe. But one day, man, I'm going to get out. And when I do, I'm going to come after you and your family." The guy winced in pain, clenching his teeth. "You married? Girlfriend, maybe? What about a daughter? Yeah, I bet you have a daughter. Trust me, she won't remember much when I'm done with her."

Reznick said nothing, only gripped his gun tighter.

The guy's white teeth were exposed as he smiled. "I can't wait to hear the bitch scream when I meet up with her."

Reznick drilled two bullets into the man's head before the Feds even made it through the door.

Twenty-Seven

The lights from the FBI SWAT team's weapons bathed the huge industrial space, illuminating the two thugs' bodies, lying in pools of their own blood.

A SWAT guy shouted, "You OK, Jon?"

"I'm fine."

Reznick heard the soft sobs behind the plasterboard wall. He walked over, crouched down on his hands and knees, and stared into the dark space. He could just make out a shivering young woman, clearly in shock, staring back at him. "Camila Perez?"

"Please don't hurt me."

"FBI, ma'am. It's OK, you're safe now."

"Is it over?" she whispered. "I don't know if I can trust you."

"It's over. You're safe. And yes, you can trust me. Don't be afraid."

Reznick reached in, grabbed her hand, and hauled her out of the cramped space. She flung her arms around his neck and began wailing.

"I thought they were going to kill me!" she said.

Reznick extricated himself from her tight embrace. "It's over. I swear to God it's over."

"I thought I was going to die!" Perez turned around and caught sight of the dead bodies on the ground. She screamed, an animalistic scream, echoing around the brick walls of the warehouse. Then she began to flail around, as if she were still fighting for her life. The delayed acute shock had kicked in. She had become hysterical.

Reznick held her arms tight to restrain her. "It's over! Do you hear me? You're safe."

"I want to see Leon!"

He didn't relish telling her that Cortez, even if he made a miraculous recovery from his overdose and got clean, was going to lose his job at the FBI and go to jail, so he elected to conceal that news from her at that moment. That wasn't his concern. "Leon is alive. And he is safe. Do you understand what I'm saying?"

The woman was breathing hard, struggling to get on top of the fear and terror she had suppressed while hiding.

Reznick turned to face the SWAT team. They were spreading out, making sure the area was secure. He signaled to the SWAT leader for the woman to be taken out of the warehouse. "Go with them," he said. "Let's get you out of here."

"Thank you," she said. "Thank you so much. God have mercy on your soul."

Reznick watched as Camila Perez was led out of the warehouse. The SWAT team leader approached, his radio crackling to life. He waited until Perez had been led out of the huge space before he fixed his gaze on Reznick. "What the fucking hell just happened here? The guy had surrendered. I heard it all. He wasn't a threat."

"He was in my eyes. That's why he was neutralized."

"Neutralized? We're not on the battlefield."

"I disagree. The fucker was hunting her down. As was his friend. They needed to be taken down."

The SWAT guy shook his head. "Are you out of your mind? The guy was begging for his life . . . He was no longer a threat."

"Bullshit."

"You killed him in cold blood."

Reznick took a step forward and squared up to the guy. "Look, I'm not going to get into some discussion about ethics with you. The guy was a threat. A real threat. If you heard it all, then you heard that part too. The guy was neutralized. End of story."

"You had him on the ground. He had been disarmed."

"Couldn't say for sure, it was too dark."

"I can't believe what I'm hearing."

"I don't give a shit about that. I made sure the girl lived. I also made sure I wasn't killed, or your guys. You will go home to your families tonight. And those thugs will not terrorize one more person in New York tonight, tomorrow, or ever."

"That's not the way we do things."

"Yeah, well, maybe you need to change that."

"What the hell does that mean?"

"It means, sometimes, you shouldn't worry about such bullshit. Neutralize the threat, then move on."

"There are rules for a reason."

"Rules? What fucking rules? Don't give me that. You think that worthless piece of shit operated with rules? There are no rules for gang-bangers like that. That's what they thrive on."

"Jon, if you operate under the jurisdiction of the FBI, there are rules. I operate under those rules of engagement."

"Good for you."

"We could have arrested him, taken him in. It's called due process."

"And what about when he's put in jail, and he's sending out notes to his buddies to continue their operations? To go after my daughter? To go after those of us who caught him, like those bastards did at Yankee Stadium this morning? Have you ever thought of that?"

"I have to write this up, Jon. I have to say what I heard. And it won't look good."

"You must have me confused with someone who gives a fuck. You worry about things looking good if you have to. Meanwhile, I'll just be the crazy fucker who took out those two Aryan Brotherhood psychopaths up in the Bronx. And one of their pals on Long Island this afternoon. Now these bastards. I'm having a really shitty day. Don't give me lectures about what I should or shouldn't have done."

"This isn't finished. Not by a long shot."

Reznick brushed past the guy and his SWAT colleagues, made his way downstairs to a waiting SUV. He climbed in the back seat and slammed the door shut.

His adrenaline was still pumping after the chase through the warehouse. He was content that the first MS-13 thug had to be taken down after he'd discovered Perez's hiding place. But the second guy, it was true, he could have spared. He could have waited for SWAT to cuff him and lead him away.

He knew he had crossed a line. He should have held back. He should have shown restraint. But he hadn't. Why?

Maybe he wanted to play judge, jury, and executioner. Then again, maybe he was just so sick of homicidal dirtbags that he had decided to give them a taste of their own medicine. The assassinations today had been planned from inside prison. It was naive to think that locking up guys like that was enough to stop them.

Was he at the end of his rope? Was he not thinking straight? Was he just running on empty? Or was it, perhaps, the threats to harm his daughter? Was that it? Was that what had pushed him over the edge? He didn't know if the guy was bluffing. Maybe he was. But in that split second, Reznick felt something, a force inside him, deep down in his soul, ignite. The mocking eyes of the gangbanger, lying on the ground, seemed to touch a nerve. A raw nerve. He didn't even think. He had become a machine. A killing machine.

Reznick knew he needed to take a closer, harder look at himself. His own motivations. Was something in him coming apart? Was he losing control?

The more he thought about it, the more he wondered if Cortez's story might serve as a warning. A good guy who'd gone bad. And the reason? Drug dependency. Was that it? Maybe it was part of the reason. Reznick was no opiate user like Cortez. But he thought about the Dexedrine. He couldn't remember a day when he wasn't speeding. He had long forgotten why he popped them when he wasn't working. Day in, day out. Stimulated, energized, alert. The feelings of euphoria. Confidence. The feeling he could do anything, that he was invincible. It was like being on a knife edge all the time. The need for speed. The adrenaline coursing through his veins.

Was he more like Cortez than he cared to imagine? Had the amphetamines and rage numbed his senses? And had it culminated in him losing control? Cortez had lost control. Of his life. His job. Everything. And all because of an addiction that had gotten out of hand. Cortez had crossed a line. But the reality was so had Reznick.

He didn't need to kill the gangbanger in cold blood. But he did it. He knew the importance of restraint. He'd had time to wait for the FBI SWAT team. But he had deliberately taken the law into his own hands. It was like a scene he'd witnessed in Iraq countless times. Iraqis in flexcuffs shot in the head. Cold blood. Eye for an eye. It was biblical justice. But he wasn't in a war. He was home, on American soil. The war was over. But somewhere deep inside Reznick, a war raged on. Threatening to engulf not only him but anyone whose path he crossed.

Maybe he didn't care whether he lived or died. Was that it? Did he have a death wish? He didn't seem to mind the grief he was giving Meyerstein. He knew she had his back against those in the highest echelons of the FBI who wanted him out. But maybe the truth was he didn't give a damn anymore.

Why was that? Was he past caring? Had he seen so much bloodshed and killings over the years that it had begun to eat away at the very fiber of his soul? It was like a descent into some kind of madness. He felt as if he were on a runaway train. And nothing and no one could stop it. Only death.

Except death was his game.

His cell phone rang, snapping him out of his contemplative mood. Reznick pulled it from his jeans pocket.

"Good job," Meyerstein said when he answered.

"I don't think your SWAT guy thought so."

"What do you mean?"

Reznick explained how he had taken out the second of the two gangbangers. "It's not pretty, I know."

"Jesus, Jon."

"Look, I understand there are protocols. But these guys were hunting that girl. He threatened Lauren."

"You killed him in cold blood?"

"Yes, I did. It is what it is."

Meyerstein was quiet for a few moments. "What the hell is wrong with you? Don't you get it? That's not how it works. Not now, not ever. Goddamn you, Jon. Why the hell would you do that?"

"Things happen. It was dark."

"Do you understand what will happen now? The SWAT guy will file a report. And they'll throw the book at you. You'll be investigated. You'll face charges. The government and the FBI will have to carry out separate investigations into your actions. This will not end well for you, Jon."

"I'm well aware of that. But I'll deal with it when the time comes."

"Jon, this is not fucking Delta Force. We're not behind enemy lines, goddamn it."

"Sometimes it feels like it. Not sure who the enemy really is."

"What the hell are you talking about? Do you think I'm the enemy? Do you, Jon?"

Reznick said nothing.

"I'm not the enemy, Jon. Not now, not ever."

"I know that."

"You know you'll have to answer questions about this later."

"Later is fine with me."

They were silent for a moment, the events of the day weighing on both of them. "Anyway," Meyerstein said, "thank God you found her safe. And you got rid of those two crazies. But there will have to be a reckoning for what happened, make no mistake. Goddamn it, Jon."

Reznick sighed.

"I've got to be honest, I feel like I'm losing track of what's going on today."

"I thought you had everything figured out, Martha. Super organized, spreadsheets orderly, et cetera."

"That goes out the window on days like this, let me tell you."

Reznick got quiet.

"Jon, I hope you don't mind. I tried to contact Lauren."

"I don't mind at all."

"I know you were worried about her. So I texted her."

"What did she say?"

Meyerstein sighed. "She told me she's in Times Square. She's a smart girl, Jon."

"I know she is."

"She can handle herself."

"I know she can . . . The problem is Todd O'Keefe is in the city tonight, I guarantee it."

"You think he's going to resurface in Times Square?"

"Like I said before, this isn't over. This isn't anywhere close to over."

Twenty-Eight

Darkness had fallen over lower Manhattan.

Meyerstein was alone in the conference room, staring out the windows of the twenty-sixth floor, contemplating the horrific events of the day. She gazed at the lights on in the offices and apartments that occupied the skyscrapers all around. She could just make out what looked like a young woman, sitting at her kitchen table, tapping away on her laptop in an adjacent residential tower. She wondered what the woman did for a living. Was she working on the Fourth of July? Was she emailing friends and family with news of her whereabouts on such a terrible day for New York City?

The sound of fireworks exploding in the distance temporarily snapped her out of her thoughts. Like gunfire. And again. Then the Manhattan sky lit up. Bathed in dark purples and bright reds as the pyrotechnics illuminated the night. She thought of the millions of people watching on TV. And the hundreds of thousands watching in and around New York City after a dark, dark day for the city.

She checked her watch. It was 9:26 p.m.

Her thoughts turned to her family back in DC. She hadn't spoken to them since that morning, shortly after the attacks had begun outside Yankee Stadium. She had messaged her teenage children and her saint of a mother, who was looking after her kids while she was away. And she'd told them not to worry. But she knew that like most people, having seen the images and footage on the news, worry they would. She even thought of her former husband, a professor. He was still shacked up with a student of his. The young woman he had dumped Meyerstein for. It hurt. Deeply. The shock had been almost too much to bear. The deception had cut deep. And the wounds hadn't healed yet. She wondered what they were doing at this moment. Were they enjoying a vacation in the Hamptons? She knew he borrowed a small beach house, owned by two old friends of his, in Montauk. She wondered if he was there, with *her*, enjoying a romantic meal for two. Walking on the moonlit beach, bottle of wine in hand, bathed in the beam of the Montauk lighthouse. Meanwhile, she was alone, staring out into the night.

She pushed her personal thoughts to one side. The more she tried to piece together the chain of that day's events, the angrier she got, thinking about the deeply compromised Leon Cortez, who was now dead. It was unfathomable that he had put lives at risk, including his fiancée's, and threatened highly sensitive investigations. Perhaps irreparably.

She had known of only one agent in all her time who had succumbed to drug addiction. And he was a rookie, a high-flying Penn State graduate who had joined the FBI at the same time as her.

Her cell phone rang, the sudden noise startling her.

"Meyerstein speaking," she said.

"Martha, sorry to bother you on a day like this. It's Steve Conti, counsel for the Office of Professional Responsibility."

"Steve, thanks for calling back. Did you look over my notes on the meeting with Leon Cortez?"

"Just finished. I see Special Agent Cortez signed off on the notes too."

Meyerstein sighed. "Now he's dead."

"I just heard. What a fucking mess."

"Indeed. He didn't try and hide anything. Completely up-front when asked to explain."

"How the hell did this all come out today?"

Meyerstein sighed. "Purely by chance. A guy who works for us, a consultant, was out in Southampton. Speaking to the eldest O'Keefe brother. The brother mentioned that he had passed on his concerns directly to Special Agent Cortez."

"This is explosive stuff."

"You don't have to tell me. I know exactly how this will be covered in the media if it gets out. And once the social media circus starts up, the FBI will be eviscerated."

"Let's not even go there."

"So, Steve, do you need anything else from us at this stage?"

"The fiancée is . . ."

"Being interviewed by two special agents as we speak. We got to her just in time."

"And she doesn't know he's dead."

"Not yet."

"Might be best if we get her down to DC. I don't want her doing anything crazy."

"I have no objection to that, at least once we have her statement."

"There's another thing: I'm reading that she works at JFK. Is that right?"

"Yes, I believe so. Customs."

"Shit. We'll have to dig into whether she facilitated any smuggling operations. Thanks, Martha. I'll be in touch if I need anything else."

Meyerstein ended the call. She stared out at the lights piercing the gathering gloom. She could only imagine the despair in the homes of the families of the ten slain NYPD officers. Down on those New York streets, they'd drawn their last breath as they served the city. Mown down by three maniacs.

There were so many questions still to be answered about these killings. And the questions just seemed to be mounting, including what the FBI's part was in the whole terrible chain of events.

Meyerstein was struggling to come to terms with the bad decisions and poor choices of one corrupt special agent. But it was all linked to poor oversight within the New York field office. She could barely believe that the FBI had received a specific tip-off from Robert O'Keefe. A tip-off that could have exposed the whole conspiracy. A chance to arrest the O'Keefes. The decision by Cortez to bury Robert O'Keefe's call was unforgivable, and would almost certainly lead to House and Senate Intelligence Committee inquiries. She would be called to testify. It wouldn't be pretty. It would be brutal. And all captured on live national TV.

Meyerstein considered her earlier telephone conversation with Reznick. He'd said that Greer, before he was gunned down, had specifically mentioned Campbell as being a powerful player in the Aryan Brotherhood. A conduit between them and MS-13. But also, perhaps, a US intelligence asset with links to the Mexican drug cartels.

Was the late Charlie Campbell being protected as a DEA asset? Were they pulling the strings? She could well imagine that if Campbell had had knowledge of drugs traveling from Mexico on certain routes up to New York, the DEA would have wanted to protect such a vital source. Was Campbell informing on the cartels, bringing back intel to the DEA? But also the CIA?

Had the Agency or the DEA, or maybe both, pressured the NYPD to drop any investigation into Campbell or the O'Keefes, to protect operations going on in Mexico? Had they been keeping the NYPD out of the loop? But some NYPD narcs had taken things into their own hands, finally busting Charlie Campbell. She knew it was possible. Perhaps even likely.

Meyerstein could see Cortez was just a small piece of the puzzle. It would take months to untangle the whole sorry mess. Maybe years. Maybe they'd never get to the bottom of it. It felt as if they were firefighting: always on defense, reacting to events as they unfolded.

She could only imagine how it would look if the story came out. But it would have to come out. Otherwise that would be just another cover-up.

What was also clear was that Reznick had killed one of the MS-13 guys in cold blood. She knew there would be ramifications.

Meyerstein was loath to admit it, but she was in awe of Reznick. She played by the rules, and while she might have disapproved of Reznick's killer instincts, she couldn't avoid the fact that his methods cut through a lot of niceties. A lot of bureaucracy. FBI special agents could use deadly force, but only when the agent had a reasonable belief that the subject posed an imminent danger of death or serious physical injury. A verbal warning, if feasible, should be given before any use of deadly force.

Reznick would have to be held accountable. But Meyerstein knew that she would never testify against him in such circumstances. The city owed Reznick a huge debt. He was out there hunting those bastards down. Himself. One man.

Besides, Meyerstein admitted, she was finding it hard to reconcile the idealistic young woman she had been when she joined the FBI with the hard-bitten assistant director who realized that sometimes in life, things get messy. Lines get blurred. In this particular case, what was the alternative? The surviving gangbanger goes to prison, gets out in a few years, recommencing his crimes, killing, and intimidation, dealing drugs and murdering innocents?

Forget the law; what about justice?

Meyerstein knew full well the end-justifies-the-means approach could not, ordinarily, be endorsed. It was not only unethical and unlawful; it wasn't the right way for the FBI or any law enforcement agency in the twenty-first century to act. But still, she knew the job had changed her once deeply held views.

She felt as if her by-the-book beliefs were slowly eroding. Maybe because of Reznick's influence and how he operated. But then maybe it was the years of seeing criminality in all its guises and permutations—whether terrorism, violence, homicide, or whatnot—and how the bad guys didn't care if they were put away for years or decades. There were always more to take their place.

Meyerstein could see that Reznick's consultant status within the FBI, which she had introduced, might become untenable. She wondered if her friendship with Reznick was clouding her judgment. That didn't sit right with her. Everyone had to work under the same rules. The same laws. But the reality was she was the one allowing Reznick to operate with impunity.

She felt deeply torn as to how to deal with Reznick. On the one hand, she admired his bravery and maverick approach to often sensitive operations. He got results. Each and every time. But on the other hand, she was the one allowing him to become a law unto himself. She was the one allowing him to continually go rogue.

Meyerstein saw that her deployment of Reznick, while getting results, had compromised her own role at the FBI. She was letting his actions go unchecked. He wasn't being held accountable. And she knew some of her colleagues were talking about her. Spreading rumors and imagining reasons she let Reznick get away with so much. None of it was true. But the gossip gnawed at her.

She wanted to be seen for what she was: a tough, smart FBI assistant director who was respected in the intelligence community. She wondered why none of her male counterparts were accused of similar transgressions. It was common knowledge in the Hoover Building that Associate Deputy Director Ted Ramirez was carrying on with a pretty FBI SWAT team member, Roberta Stevens. But as far as Meyerstein knew, there had been no insinuation about Ramirez's ability to do the job. It was a double standard. However, as a woman, she had long since grown accustomed to male colleagues being given the benefit of the doubt in the workplace. But to be fair, their misgivings weren't only about Meyerstein's close relationship with Reznick. They were also about how she deployed Reznick, a known assassin who used to work for the Agency. She sensed that her use of the unorthodox Reznick was beginning to erode some of the trust, goodwill, and respect from her colleagues that she had built up over the years. That bothered her. A lot. So what was she going to do about it? Was it time to pull the plug on Jon Reznick?

The more she thought about it, the more she wondered if her FBI colleagues might be right. She was shielding Reznick time and time again when his actions crossed into illegality, threatening to derail investigations. She was taking the flak for him. But why?

Was it her and not just Reznick who had crossed a line? Maybe it was more personal for her than she had imagined. All of a sudden, it dawned on her. She did care about him. Far more than she'd probably care to admit. Sometimes at the end of a hard day at the office, the children in bed, she would think of Reznick as she relaxed with a glass of wine. She invariably wondered where he was. What was he up to? The relationship appeared, on the surface, to be purely business. But she had begun to wonder if her high-powered job at the FBI was compatible with a character like Jon Reznick. Was she jeopardizing her career by remaining so close to him?

The fact was, to her, Jon Reznick was indispensable. Not only in the classified investigations she worked on, but in her life. He didn't walk away when the going got tough. He didn't bullshit. He was strong. And he wasn't interested in the machinations of power. She liked that about him. He was a lone wolf. A hunter. And it was that single-mindedness and focus, not to mention his self-deprecation, she found so appealing.

Meyerstein had read his file. She knew his psychological profile. She sensed he wasn't a guy that sent flowers, unlike her ex-husband. That didn't bother her in the slightest. But she could see that she didn't want to be without Reznick in her life. Even just to hear his voice on the phone. But she had serious concerns about his mental state. She worried that he was more damaged than she realized. He had issues.

Serious issues. His behavior greatly troubled her. She felt uncomfortable with his use of amphetamines. She knew he was using drugs all the time. He didn't bother to hide it from her. She'd lost count of the number of times he had knocked back two Dexedrine with a cup of coffee, or bottle of water, during an operation. She'd noticed, but she'd never said anything. She had always figured that Jon knew what he was doing. But after what had happened with Cortez . . . now she wasn't so sure. Had his drug use played a part in the killing of the MS-13 member in Gowanus earlier? Was he trigger-happy? What could she do about it? Would he listen to her? What was she to him, after all? His boss? Or something more? She made a mental note to talk to him about that. The drug might help his performance, but had it begun to impair his judgment? While amphetamines would no doubt make him alert and poised to meet any threat, the downsides, of which there were many, included mood swings and, in rare cases, psychosis.

Meyerstein reflected on all of this for a few moments. She had never taken a step back to realize how long she had put up with his drug use. Had turned a blind eye to it, because she didn't want to see it. Didn't want to know.

Not to mention how her attitude toward her work had changed in the time since she'd known Jon Reznick. Her mind-set had gone from by-the-book FBI operations to high risk. Her views were changing too. She had developed a skin as thick as a rhino's since she'd been working with Reznick. He didn't give a shit about what people thought. And she had begun to feel much the same about the politics within the FBI.

She wondered sometimes what her career had all been for. The sacrifices, the time away from her family, the loneliness, and the specter of plots and conspiracies her team had investigated, which seemed to leave an indelible mark on her. The feelings of emptiness on days like this. It reminded her of the terrible hours and days after 9/11. The shock of such a monumental attack on US soil, less than a mile from where she

J. B. Turner

was now in lower Manhattan, still lingered. She could see the Freedom Tower glistening in the moonlight.

It was as if every bad day at the office, every disappointment and every sliver of anger that had lain dormant inside her for years, was now being stoked up inside her.

Meyerstein felt like a different woman than in her younger days. Her idealism was retreating into the mists of time. She thought of her precious children, her mother, back in DC. She wanted to hold them tight at that moment. To hug them. To reassure them.

That wasn't an option now for the families of the slain NYPD officers. The pain, the suffering, would be enduring. The heartbreak. She thought of the knock at the door that each and every wife, husband, or partner of one of the dead NYPD cops would have gotten that day. To listen to a solemn-faced colleague telling them, as they stood on their doorstep on July 4, the gut-wrenching news that their loved one would not be home that night. Or ever again. From now until the day that they themselves died, the Fourth of July would not be a day of celebration. It would be a day of grief.

Meyerstein sighed, realizing she'd lost herself in dark thoughts. She needed to snap out of it. She turned around and faced the huge TV screens in the conference room. Fox News and CNN were playing. Shots of vigils outside Yankee Stadium and in the Financial District. And one just off Times Square. Lingering close-ups of grim-faced New York police officers standing guard.

She thought again of Lauren Reznick, down there, among the crowd of idealistic young men and women, lighting candles, praying for peace.

Meanwhile, out on the streets, working in the shadows, Lauren's father was neutralizing each and every threat he encountered. Unseen. Unloved. Unbowed. She cared for Jon Reznick. She imagined how she would react to the news of him being shot. Maybe even killed. She worried about him. A lot. But unlike her colleagues, she appreciated the serious risks Reznick took and the deep sacrifices he made for America. He put himself on the line. Time after time. He didn't back down. She loved that about him.

The phone on her desk rang. She was sorely tempted to just let it be. But she never could.

"Yeah, Meyerstein speaking."

"Assistant Director Meyerstein . . ." The voice belonged to Bobby Levinson, a nervous FBI analyst within the Counterterrorism Center in McLean.

"What is it, Bobby?"

"Channel thirty-two, turn to channel thirty-two."

Meyerstein picked up the remote and keyed in the number. Four separate still images showed what looked like Todd O'Keefe at the wheel of a pickup, date-stamped three minutes earlier. "Is that him?"

"One hundred percent sure."

"Where?"

"South of the Theater District. He was picked up by four different NYPD cameras."

"Have we alerted police, Homeland Security?"

"Everyone."

"But where is he now?"

"Thirty seconds ago was the last visual. NYPD Emergency Service Units and undercover units are on it."

"Do we think he's targeting the vigil in Times Square?"

"We don't know for sure. We do know there are a lot of police there."

"Good work, Bobby. But we need to intercept him. Get on it."

Meyerstein ended the call and updated the Director, who would then inform the President's national security adviser. She switched channels and looked at news coverage of the vigil in Times Square. She wondered if they shouldn't just try and clear Times Square. But she knew that was almost logistically impossible. The number of people, the size of the area. It would cause mass panic.

She picked up her cell phone and called Reznick and updated him.

"We need to clear the area," he said.

"I considered that," she said. "Would take hours at best. There would be panic, people getting crushed, and in the mayhem, you could guarantee that O'Keefe would carry out another attack and also manage to escape."

"My daughter is there."

Meyerstein rubbed her temple. "I know, Jon. If I wasn't working here, I'd head straight there and get her out immediately myself."

"Can't the NYPD, plainclothes, whoever, just get down there and gradually start easing people away from the area?"

"I think they're doing that, but you know what people are like. They're stubborn. And I've just seen surveillance footage in and around Times Square, and it's rarely looked busier. It's impossible without just driving them off the streets. But doing so also might result in panic, a stampede, God knows what."

"Makes sense. I get that. Heart attacks, anxiety, all that."

"Precisely. Jon, I know you don't want to hear this, but you've earned a serious rest. You need to call it a day and we'll handle it."

There was silence on the other end of the line.

"Jon, are you still there?"

"Yeah, I'm still here."

"Did you hear what I said?"

"I heard." Reznick paused. "Martha, he's still on the loose, and my daughter is down there. I'm not leaving until this is over."

Meyerstein sighed. "Jon, you're running on empty."

"I'm fine. Trust me. Listen, can you do me a favor?"

"What kind of favor?"

"Get me embedded with an NYPD Emergency Service Unit. I don't think I'm the flavor of the month with FBI SWAT. Well, at least with their leader."

"We've got Times Square covered."

"I need to be there. I need to do something."

"This is irregular, Jon."

"I've been hearing a lot of that today, Martha, trust me."

She wondered if it was wise to put Reznick in the middle of it all, especially after the day he'd had. "My concern is you're flat-out exhausted."

"Let me worry about that."

Meyerstein sighed. "OK, leave it to me."

"Appreciate that. One more thing."

"What?"

"I need someone to find Lauren. I've tried calling her. She's not answering."

Meyerstein stared at the screen where CNN was covering the vigil close to the middle of Times Square. "I'll do my best. But Jon?"

"What?"

"Be careful. This guy is not going to go down without a fight."

"That's fine. Neither am I."

Twenty-Nine

Reznick was dropped off with an NYPD Emergency Service Unit, three blocks from Times Square. Then he was given a bulletproof vest and a headset that hooked him up with all the other members of the group. But he was also able to receive direct messages from the FBI tactical command HQ.

He climbed into the back of the Lenco BearCat armored personnel carrier, eating a slice of pizza, washed down with a bottle of cold water. The day's exertions had taken a lot out of him.

Reznick felt drained. He really needed to rest. Recharge his batteries. Sleep. He felt his mind drifting, still processing what had happened, not as sharp as he needed it to be. Not by a long shot.

A huge ESU guy sat down with him and introduced himself. "Danny Fogerty," he said, extending his hand.

Reznick shook his hand. "Hey, Danny."

"Just wanted to say, real privilege to have you with us. I believe you know a friend of mine, Detective Acosta, Nineteenth Precinct."

"Yeah, sure, I remember her well. How is she?"

"She's good. She told me all about what happened to your daughter last year, and how you took down that UN diplomat."

Reznick sighed. "A lot of other people were involved in that, Danny. But nice of you to say so."

Fogerty nodded. "I used to work in and around the United Nations, many years ago, as a patrol cop. Let me just say, I'm with you. A sorrier bunch of people I never had the misfortune to meet."

"Hey, that was then, this is now. We need to focus on this Todd O'Keefe. What do you say?"

Fogerty cleared his throat and leaned in close. "I'm also hearing you took down the crew in the Bronx this morning? That's awesome, man. Did you really do that?"

Reznick finished eating his pizza, wiped his mouth with a napkin, and dropped it on the floor. He liked Fogerty. But he didn't have any wish to elaborate on what had happened earlier that day. Besides, he always felt slightly uncomfortable getting a pat on the back for the things he did. He just wanted to get the job done and go home.

"Well, I just wanted you to know I really admire that."

"Appreciate that, thanks. So, what's the latest intel? You want to bring me up to speed?"

"They're assuming O'Keefe has dumped his vehicle and is blending in with the crowds. There are countless undercover cops looking for him. But it's like finding a needle in a haystack."

"What about vantage points?"

"We've got snipers on rooftops."

Reznick got quiet for a few moments, again thinking of Lauren. "That's good."

"Anyway, it's a pleasure to finally meet you."

"Likewise." Reznick felt a wave of tiredness wash over him. He needed something to pep him up. He reached into his back pocket and took out a tinfoil pack of Dexedrine, squeezed out four pills, and popped them in his mouth. He washed them down with the water. He knew it was bad for his mind and body. He really needed to get clean. Maybe at least cut down on his amphetamine intake. He needed to quiet his mind. Curb the fires raging within him. Taking the pills was like pouring kerosene on smoldering ashes. It needed to stop. Somehow. Sometime.

"What's that you're taking, man?" Fogerty asked.

"Vitamins."

"Bullshit, that's not vitamins."

Reznick stared at Fogerty and smiled. "Something to keep me awake. That's all."

"That give you an edge?"

"Keeps me going. It's been a long, long day."

"You think we'll get him tonight?"

"We have to, or there are going to be more dead cops on the streets of New York."

Thirty

O'Keefe disappeared down some stairs and into the bowels of Penn Station. He wore a backpack as he headed to a restroom. He stood in front of the mirror and looked at his grizzled, unkempt appearance, his dirty clothes. He unzipped the backpack and took out the toiletries bag, complete with a razor and shaving gel. He rubbed the gel into his beard until it was a thick lather. Then with great care, he began to shave the six-month growth from his face. When he was finished, he splashed cold water on his cheeks, wiping away the excess foam with paper towels.

He took off his dirty shirt and threw it on the floor. He opened the backpack wider and pulled out the fresh set of clothes. New white shirt, jeans, black Nike sneakers, and a navy blazer. Then he put on a black Yankees hat.

He stared at his reflection and grinned. He looked like a new person. The AB symbols and tattoos were hidden. He knew the Brotherhood had some smart people in their ranks, including ex-military who knew about getting around and trying to evade capture.

O'Keefe put on a pair of aviator shades. He stared at himself. He almost burst out laughing at how different he looked. He ditched the bag in a stall. Then he walked out of the restroom and took an elevator to the ground level.

The crowds were swarming all around him like shoals of fish. He headed out of the station and into the humid night air. A couple blocks later, he found a Dunkin' Donuts. He was in desperate need of sustenance. He ordered two donuts and a sweet white coffee. It tasted great. He felt his sugar levels rising.

The place was packed, people talking loudly. The sound of some hip-hop shit punctuated the chatter. He turned around and saw a black kid with silver Beats headphones hanging around his neck. The music he was listening to was spilling out for everyone to hear. The kid began harassing and haranguing the black woman behind the counter about having to wait in line.

O'Keefe was tempted to walk up to the arrogant little fuck and stab him in the neck. He'd lost count of the number of times a loudmouth inmate had gotten shanked for talking big. The codes of conduct inside were different. But out on the street, no one was constrained. You could act how you wanted without any consequences.

He picked up a napkin and wiped the sugar and dregs of coffee from his lips. On his way out he brushed past the loud black kid, who looked surprised. He shot the kid a glance and he averted his gaze. The loudmouth wasn't as dumb as he looked.

O'Keefe went next door to a luggage storage facility. He handed over his ticket and signed for a suitcase that had been dropped off for him. The Hispanic kid behind the counter cheerfully handed over the large Samsonite with wheels. He handed the boy fifty dollars, told him to keep the change.

"Thank you, sir," he said.

O'Keefe grinned. "Buy your mother something nice."

The kid smiled back. "Yeah, I will, thanks."

O'Keefe walked a few blocks, pulling the case behind him. He checked into a one-star hostel that had been carefully selected. The filthy lobby smelled of stale smoke, cooking oil, and a faint whiff of hashish.

The girl behind the desk was chewing on some gum. She said it would be forty-five dollars for his room.

O'Keefe could only imagine the shithole room he'd get for that price. He paid in cash and took the elevator to his squalid twelfth-floor room. Sticky carpet—booze had been spilled and never cleaned. He locked the door and looked out of the window. The neon lights of Times Square shone a few hundred yards away.

He shut the curtains and switched on Fox News. It was wall-to-wall coverage of the attacks. Faces of his two older brothers again on the screen. The more he saw them, the more tense he felt.

O'Keefe felt a raw anger stirring within him. A black anger. It had abated since he had killed the two female cops. But the sight of his brothers' faces on TV had triggered something deep within him again.

O'Keefe knew the net would be closing in on him soon. He could sense it. He knew the license plate readers around the city would all be on the lookout. He knew face-recognition technology could find him. Or perhaps it would just be down to bad luck. But from the moment the AB had given the order to avenge Charlie Campbell, O'Keefe had known this day would arrive. This precise moment. Just him alone. It was his responsibility. He faced it with pride that he was part of it, but also that he was helping the AB and his two brothers avenge a good man. A legend.

O'Keefe lay back on the bed, listening to the voices of the newscasters droning on. He began to collect his thoughts. His mind flashed back to the night that his eldest brother had left. His fearsome stepfather had gathered the three remaining brothers for a "man's meeting" in the nearby woods. So they could talk without their mother overhearing anything. They were teenagers. Wild. Rebellious. But he remembered the look on his stepfather's face and the tone of his voice that night.

What had impressed Todd was that Charlie Campbell never spoke ill of Bobby, despite Bobby and Campbell not getting on from day one. Even when he left, Campbell just said to him, "I wish you all the best, son." His mother broke down and wept as she hugged her eldest son goodbye. He remembered that Bobby never looked back. He just hugged his mother, wiped away her tears, and walked out the door to the waiting cab. Their mother watched at the window, sobbing nonstop. Then she went into her room and didn't come out until the following morning. An hour after she went to bed, Charlie took Todd and his brothers into the woods. And what he said that night stuck with Todd. He remembered it almost verbatim, the message was so powerful to him:

You must never, ever talk about your brother in a disrespectful manner. There's a whole bunch of people that'll talk about you boys. You'll soon find that out. Maybe they'll talk about me. It might be neighbors. Maybe guys in the neighborhood. And that's fine. But we do not, as a family, bad-mouth Bobby. Not now, not ever. I loved Bobby, and I still love him. I know you love Bobby too. He's your blood. I've tried my best. But he's looking for a different sort of life. Maybe in the big city he'll find it. And I hope he does well. But you boys, while he has walked out on the family, never talk about him, unless it's to talk fondly. Don't ever forget that. But there's something else. You need to know that I will never walk away from you boys. I will lay down my life to protect you and your mother. I swear, I will never desert you.

Charlie Campbell was true to his word. He never did desert them. He was a bad-to-the-bone motherfucker. But he was always nice to their mother. And he was great with them. They paid attention to him. He demanded it. Todd listened in rapt amazement as Campbell talked of how a man should carry himself. How he should stand up for what he believed in. He believed in blood oaths. It was a given that if someone did harm to their "blood," vengeance had to be exacted.

He remembered hearing the news about Charlie's death. A phone call from his mother. Her voice was a whisper, as if she were afraid someone would overhear her. It was tinged with anger. Regret. She was going to be alone again. And the money might very well dry up. She had put away twenty or thirty thousand dollars, she had once confided, in a safe-deposit box. Money Charlie had made from his "work." O'Keefe knew the money would be used up within weeks. Maybe months if she was lucky. His mother was never good with money.

He thought of his mother now. How she had to be feeling. He imagined she would be looking out of the kitchen window. That's how he always remembered her. Watching and waiting for her blood. Like a sentinel. He wanted to call her. He could only imagine the despair she was feeling. The depths of darkness to which she must have plummeted. But she wouldn't understand their motivations. It was about honor. Blood and honor. Besides, he knew the Feds would either be ransacking her home or have the line bugged by now. She would have seen the news. And she would be praying to God, asking how her boys could have been the snipers. It wouldn't make sense to her. She knew they were no angels. They'd all been to prison. But she never did understand, or want to understand, the extent and ramifications of Charlie Campbell's involvement in white prison gang culture.

By the end of the day, his mother would have lost three of her boys. Only Bobby, the smart one, the oldest brother, would be left. Todd had always liked Bobby. He remembered Bobby liked to read. Day-old copies of the *New York Times*, *National Geographic* magazines that Campbell bought, or library books—mostly biographies of long-dead economists. Todd sometimes sat down beside him and looked at the pictures in the paper, leaning over his shoulder. Bobby never minded. But Bobby did mind Charlie. It was as if everything Charlie did—the way he ate, the way he talked, the things he talked about—infuriated Bobby. The day Bobby moved out, Todd could see the look of emptiness in his mother's eyes. A little part of her died that day.

The three remaining brothers just did as Charlie said. They never talked badly of Bobby. They didn't want to demean their brother's memory. They knew they were simply different from him.

His cell phone rang, stirring Todd from his memories.

"Mr. O'Keefe," drawled Mills.

Todd sat up. "How you doing?"

"I thought you'd like to hear some news. Some news that just came my way in the last five minutes."

"I'm listening."

"Just heard that the attorney general for New York has had a change of plans. Will be getting dropped off at the Theodore Building, three blocks from you, in the next few minutes. Emergency meeting with his advisers in a private meeting room within the law firm Strauss and Strauss, apparently."

"Go on."

"I know that area well. And I also know that if you go to the top of a nearby Midtown parking garage, where I used to do some dealing, there is a perfect line of sight from the top level to the building entrance, due west."

"Due west, huh? How do you know he'll be there?"

"People tell me things. Especially when they know their loved ones could be killed."

"Are we positive about this?"

"Oh yeah. He's going to be driven there and dropped off out front. They got him out of his office in lower Manhattan. He's en route, I've been told. You might have time. Obviously I don't want to put pressure on you, son. The main focus should be the last phase of the operation. But I thought you'd want to know."

"Who's protecting him?"

"That's the beauty of it. New York's finest. Couple of plainclothes cops. The vehicle is a black BMW SUV. Brand-new model. New York plates."

O'Keefe's mind began to picture the setup.

"It's up to you. You've already cemented your reputation, son. Charlie would've been proud."

O'Keefe felt his throat tighten. "I'm wondering what Charlie would've done in the circumstances. If he would've taken it on."

"Charlie was always full on. He pushed boundaries. Didn't ask questions. He would just do it or die trying. He was a stubborn old bastard."

"And the AG was definitely the guy who got Charlie put away and signed the order for the arrest that killed him?"

"That's the name given to us by our contact in the Agency. He's the one. Fucker got lucky not being home this afternoon."

"One final question. I'm just curious. What would you do in my shoes?"

The shot caller sighed. "That's your choice. I can't make it for you, brother."

O'Keefe felt the adrenaline begin to flow. He had heard enough. "I'll take it from here."

He ended the call. The rush felt like a freight train running through his head. And he loved it.

The first thing he did was unlock the suitcase on the bed. He opened it up. Inside was a 9mm Glock, locked and loaded. He tucked it inside his waistband. Then he put a black shirt on over it. The suitcase had a false bottom. He ripped it open and saw a backpack, which contained rifle parts and high-capacity magazines. He flung the backpack over his shoulder and checked himself in the mirror again. Shit, he could be anyone. A tourist.

O'Keefe watched as a grin enveloped his face. "Motherfucker!"

He headed out of his room, locked the door, and took the elevator to the lobby. He walked out of the crummy hotel and onto the boiling Midtown streets.

It was a short walk to the parking garage.

O'Keefe climbed the stairwell to the top level, heart beating hard. His gaze wandered around the vast concrete space. Three other cars were parked at the far side of the garage. At the other end, opposite another stairwell, was an elevator door. He scanned for the exits and entrances. He had gotten his bearings.

He kneeled down and took off the backpack. Unzipped it and pulled out the contents, quickly assembled the rifle, loaded the magazine, attached the sights.

Then he fixed it to a tripod, placed it on the perimeter wall, and scanned the area.

O'Keefe spotted the glass lobby of the Theodore Building. He waited for only a minute. Then the BMW pulled up.

The passenger in the front seat, who he assumed was a cop, got out and opened the back door.

O'Keefe stared through the crosshairs. A besuited figure with a dark tan got out, then turned his head toward the cop. It was him. The fucker who had put Charlie Campbell away all those fucking years ago. The guy who had signed the warrant for his arrest that led to his murder.

He took aim.

"Right, you son of a bitch."

O'Keefe squeezed the trigger twice. The shots rang out.

The attorney general collapsed, not moving. People screaming.

In that split second, both cops crouched over the body, out of sight.

"Fuck!"

O'Keefe ducked for cover, lying sprawled on the roof. He disassembled the tripod and rifle and put the parts into the backpack. He crawled with the backpack to the nearest dark stairwell, with only one bit of business left to attend to.

Thirty-One

Reznick's headset buzzed to life. It was Meyerstein.

"Jon, the attorney general of New York has just been assassinated."

"We heard some shots."

"The NYPD ShotSpotter system just flagged it. It's three blocks from you guys."

He looked across at Fogerty, who was pointing out that another unit already had that area covered. "So how did the shooter, whoever it is, know where the AG was going to be?"

"We're exploring the possibility of a leak somewhere."

"Martha, what the hell? I would've thought that the attorney general would have been taken somewhere ultra-secure, like a military facility."

"He didn't want to go, apparently. Thought it best to draw up a legal response to the killings with his advisers."

"Also, don't we have guys on the roofs?"

"We do, but they can't cover everything. Besides, the incident happened a few blocks away from the busiest part of Times Square."

"So he's able to take shots and get away? Just like that?"

"Not good, I know."

"You really need to try and get people out of Times Square."

"I know. The NYPD are quietly moving them north."

"It's not going to work in the time frame."

"You don't have to tell me that. We don't know his next move. But we have to do something. We absolutely cannot go on Twitter or Facebook and tell people to get off the streets. Bottom line? There are no good options to clear the streets."

"What a fucking mess," he said.

"We'll catch him. I'm confident of that. And we have hundreds of people working on this."

"Martha, there are literally tens of thousands of people walking in and around the Times Square area. I'm no good where I am. I need to be mobile."

"Jon, the situation is very fluid. It would be best if there wasn't another undercover operative trying to find him. Besides, it's a long, long shot."

Reznick's decision clicked into place. "Here's what I want. I want a discreet earpiece, lapel mic badge, and I want to get right into the heart of Times Square myself and be guided by FBI surveillance operatives as to what is happening in real time. Here, I'm just sitting, watching, and waiting."

Meyerstein sighed. "I'd really prefer it if you just stayed with the ESU guys."

"It's too reactive. Besides, these guys have no use for me. Also, another ESU is taking care of the shooter three blocks away. I need to get seriously proactive if we're going to stand a chance." There was a silence on the other end as if Meyerstein were weighing her options.

"OK," she finally said, "I can arrange that. We'll have one of our guys with you in the next five minutes. I'll be able to speak to you directly too. But listen to me. While I understand what you did out in Brooklyn, ideally we only shoot to prevent loss of life. Can you remember that?"

"That's assuming I can get near this guy. I'm guessing it must be Todd O'Keefe."

"That's what we think," Meyerstein said.

"He's like a goddamn ghost, drifting in and out of places unseen."

"We have to assume that he had insider information on the attorney general's movements. Someone within the AB is clearly calling the shots."

"One more thing," Reznick said. "I'm looking out the back of an Emergency Service Unit armored truck, and I don't hear or see any choppers."

"There should be two choppers. At least that's what I've been told."

"Negative. And a chopper is crucial for checking rooftops. Maybe high-floor windows."

"I'll get my team to check on that, Jon."

"Maybe they're up there. But I sure as hell haven't seen them or heard them."

"I'll take care of it. You take care of yourself."

Reznick ripped off the headset and bulletproof vest. He apologized to the guys for wasting their time. But they just wished him luck.

Fogerty said, "If you find him first, don't spare the fucker. He and his crew left widows all over New York."

Reznick smiled. "Take care, son. Be safe."

A few minutes later, a Fed pulled up in a car.

Reznick climbed in the front, and they sped off toward Times Square. He fitted himself with the new earpiece and lapel mic.

The Fed said, "You OK?"

Reznick shook his head. "No, I'm not OK. My daughter's out there somewhere at this vigil."

"Shit, I'm sorry, Jon."

Reznick sighed. "Can I ask you a question? How is this guy able to evade electronic surveillance and physical detection in the middle of New York City? We only get a visual on him for a brief moment, then it all goes dark."

"Do you know how many cameras the NYPD has across this city? It's literally thousands. And they're also able to call on private stakeholders, companies like Goldman Sachs, J.P. Morgan, and a host of others across the city. The NYPD Argus system is all over the city. They also have license plate readers for cars, cabs, trucks, you name it. If it moves, they should have it covered."

"So then how is this guy able to move about so freely without popping up on facial recognition or being spotted?"

"He could be staying indoors, or taking certain steps to disguise his appearance. And a lot of these cameras use wireless technology to transmit these images and footage back in real time to downtown police HQ."

"So . . . if he had a jammer in his possession, that might help?"

The Fed was quiet for a few moments. "Do we know if this guy has a jammer?"

"Nope. But I imagine if you have a device that can jam radio signals or cell phones, it could potentially be useful."

"Here's the thing. My wife is a cop. Detective in New Jersey. She told me about a guy a few months back who bought a cell phone jammer online from China. When the guy was on the subway, and someone was talking too loud, he would jam the cell phone, ending the conversation. Guy was a sociopath. But the little signal-jamming trick he pulled was how he was caught."

"Jesus Christ."

"So, it might explain why we haven't gotten him so far."

"The sooner we neutralize this fucker, the better."

"Stay safe tonight, Jon. And best of luck. Think we're going to need it."

Reznick got out of the vehicle in the heart of Times Square. Huge neon-lit billboards towered all around, advertising TVs, cell phones, and God knows what else. Tens of thousands of people thronged the sidewalks and streets. Car horns and police sirens and the hubbub of the crowd assaulted his senses. He stood, earpiece in, wearing a metallic Stars and Stripes lapel badge hiding the miniature microphone inside it. He knew that the sniper could have anyone within a square mile in his sights. The crowds jostled past, as if oblivious to the attacks earlier that day. Nothing was going to spoil their Fourth of July night. Headed to shows, concerts, bars, restaurants. The reality hit home. To clear the Times Square area and vicinity would mean shutting down New York. It might have been possible. But it would be chaotic and would almost certainly not foil whatever Todd O'Keefe had in mind that night.

As far as Reznick was concerned, Todd O'Keefe, wherever he was, was intent on taking down more cops before the night was over, or dying while he tried.

Reznick surveyed the people all around. Men and women, black and white, all sizes and demeanors. It was virtually impossible to tell the tourists and visitors from the native New Yorkers enjoying Independence Day. Traffic cops tried to keep things moving. The crowds seemed to be growing. How was that possible?

Reznick's thoughts turned to his daughter. Lauren couldn't be far from him. But where the hell was she? He spoke into the lapel badge mic. "Quick question: Where is the vigil?"

Meyerstein said, "Let me see . . . The vigil is currently two blocks south of you. At the intersection of Forty-Fourth and Broadway."

Reznick was sorely tempted to head straight there and be beside his daughter. He figured she must have been just around the corner from him when he was with the ESU. He wished he'd known, as he would definitely have headed straight there. But now he was torn whether to be with her or stay put, ready to take this fucker down.

"How you feeling, Jon?"

"I've felt better." The fact of the matter was Reznick felt agitated. O'Keefe could pop up anywhere at any moment. Every one of the thousands of people there right then was in danger. But mostly he was agitated thinking about his daughter, putting herself in harm's way when she didn't have to.

"You're worrying about Lauren, aren't you? It's natural, Jon. But she's a smart kid."

Reznick sighed. "I'd prefer if she was off the streets tonight. After what happened this morning . . ."

"She wants to exert her independence. That's a good thing, isn't it?"

"I guess."

"She'll be fine. Besides, this guy's MO seems to be cops."

"You're forgetting the attorney general."

"True."

"What possessed him to kill the attorney general? It's insane."

"We believe this is directly related to Campbell's conviction a decade ago. The AG prosecuted. But he was also the one who recently gave the go-ahead for the NYPD to arrest Campbell on drug smuggling, intimidation, and violence, under RICO. That arrest resulted in Campbell's death."

"Martha, I'm dying down here. It's just watching and waiting. It's killing me."

Meyerstein sighed. "We got some footage of O'Keefe leaving a budget hotel near Penn Station, carrying a backpack. Dropped off the grid in the last hour."

"Again? You've got to be kidding me. And he just disappeared?"

"Looks like he caught an Uber headed north on Eighth Avenue. We think Times Square is the ultimate destination. It's the busiest locale. He may be lying low after taking out the AG."

"And we don't know where those shots were fired from?"

"We have a good idea. There's a parking garage nearby, so we're wondering if this is part of a plan, the same ploy he used when he was down in lower Manhattan."

"This guy is getting help. He's not acting alone."

"We know that."

"So where the fuck is he? Is he using a signal jammer? That's what I'm thinking. The FBI driver who dropped me off mentioned the same thing."

"Look, we're working the problem, Jon."

"That's not good enough. You've got to be able to pull this guy out of a crowd. Otherwise, what's the point of all those cameras and technology?"

"It's not a perfect solution. Not yet. It's getting better."

"There are cops everywhere, and they are all sitting targets, as are those around them. And my daughter—"

"Hang on . . ."

"What?"

The silence was deafening on the other end of the line.

"Martha, what is it?"

"Stand by, Jon."

Reznick felt wired, a mixture of adrenaline and Dexedrine coursing through his veins.

"Got an update . . ."

A guy brushed past and snapped, "Why the fuck are you stopping in the middle of the sidewalk, dumb ass? This is New York, asshole."

Reznick ignored the idiot. "Martha, what the hell is going on?"

"One of our facial-recognition guys found him. In the back seat of a car, an Uber."

"So where is he?"

"We believe he left a parking garage off Thirty-Ninth and Broadway."

"Where the fuck is he right now?"

Thirty-Two

Todd O'Keefe was headed along West Forty-Third Street, backpack slung over his shoulder. He spotted a neon sign outside a shitty-looking hotel. No cameras. No surveillance. A rarity in New York.

He was certainly becoming an aficionado of crap hotel rooms in the city. He paid cash and took the elevator to the fifteenth floor, suitcase in hand. Headed down a bleak corridor with cigarette burns on the carpet. He unlocked the door and went inside. His misgivings were well founded. The smell of piss was overwhelming. He was careful to lock the door again behind him.

O'Keefe looked around. The whiff of nicotine and piss reminded him of the penitentiary. He went over to the bed. Brown and yellow flowers adorned the nylon duvet cover.

He pulled back the duvet and all the sheets to reveal the filthy mattress. Dirty brown stains like blotches on the skin. Perhaps bedbugs. Perhaps blood. Perhaps someone had shit themselves in the bed. A fleabag hotel. He had seen better conditions inside prison.

No matter, this was where it was going to go down.

O'Keefe unzipped a side pocket of the backpack. He pulled out the methamphetamine tablets. He popped ten of them, crunched them, and washed them down with some warm water from the faucet.

Within fifteen minutes, he was wired, raging, and ready for the endgame. Like a fire ablaze in his head, whipped up by hurricane-force winds. It was a good feeling. And what a great day to end it. Independence Day. Right in the heart of Gotham.

Those fuckers would pay. They would pay, alright.

O'Keefe began to pace the tiny room. He felt an itch on his arm. He began to scratch feverishly. Clawing at his forearms. He felt like he was entering a distorted, trippy nightmare from which he wouldn't emerge. Then again, maybe he would.

He picked up the remote and switched on the TV. Fox News was still showing pictures of his brothers.

He turned away.

O'Keefe got down on the floor. He began to do push-ups. Then sit-ups. He felt an insane energy within him. But he also felt a terrible, cheery malevolence begin to take hold. He looked up at the TV as he worked out. A photo of Charlie Campbell appeared.

O'Keefe smiled. He stared at the TV and thought back to his childhood. He remembered as a boy watching *Celebrity Deathmatch* on MTV with Charlie. And the Madonna videos. George Michael. They both couldn't stop laughing.

He picked up the remote and switched to MTV. Some dumb-ass hip-hop clown, throwing gang signs, bass-heavy beats, interspersed with images of the goofball knocking back champagne, surrounded by silicone chicks in bikinis. The lame wannabe tough guy would be killed in prison. No question. Probably by his own side. O'Keefe had seen bigmouth troublemakers sliced open within seconds of talking trash or talking big to some serious dudes. It never played out well.

He remembered one white guy, big name, big tough-guy reputation, New Jersey, blue-collar trash talker, walking around the yard. Swaggering, covered in tattoos. But the tattoos meant nothing. They weren't AB tattoos or Nazi Low Rider tattoos.

It was Celtic crosses, iconography, all over his neck and arms. Crosses here, there, and everywhere. Knuckles, forehead, like it meant something.

When O'Keefe casually looked across at him in the yard, the guy, who was six foot six, towering over him, looked down at him and spat at his feet. "Fuck you looking at, asshole? You want some? Huh, you wanna come ahead and get some?"

O'Keefe just stared at him, homemade shank already hidden behind his back. He was always prepared to fight. He had Charlie to thank for that.

"What the fuck is the matter with you, you little fuck? Whose bitch are you?"

A friend of the huge guy whispered in his ear.

"My friend says you might be one of the Brand," the big guy said. "You don't look like much to me. No way would the Brotherhood allow you in. You ain't got the balls."

O'Keefe smiled at him, knowing that would infuriate the hulk.

The poor fucker took a few steps forward and reached out to grab O'Keefe by the neck. O'Keefe simply parried the huge arm and thrust forward, knifing the giant in the neck. Again and again. Then down into his face. And eyes. Again. And again. The guy bled out within seconds.

No one did a fucking thing. No guards saw a thing. It was business.

The hip-hop brain-mush on the TV was relentless.

O'Keefe felt a surge of excitement through his body knowing what he was going to do. He hated the music. But he turned up the volume. The bass got louder. He felt seriously crazy. The methamphetamine was frying his brain and blood. He felt his blood pressure begin to rise. He found himself clenching his fist. Grinding his teeth. He felt the veins and muscles in his neck tightening.

Banging on the wall from upstairs as the noise vibrated through the bricks. Through the pipework.

O'Keefe ignored it for a few minutes. Once he felt hyped up, he decided to turn it down. The banging from upstairs stopped. The sound of a baby crying next door. Raised voices. Maybe a family holed up in one of the shitty rooms.

He felt as if he was possessed. And he liked it. Actually loved it.

Memories flooded back from when he was a teenager. Charlie walking him and his brothers through the woods to a makeshift firing range. He remembered the feeling when Charlie ruffled his hair.

Once you learn to fight, no one will fuck with you. Once you learn to shoot, no one will fuck with you.

A knock at the door interrupted his train of thought.

O'Keefe ignored it for a few moments.

A series of sharp knocks followed.

O'Keefe wondered who it was. He got up from the floor and looked through the peephole.

A small woman, hair tied back. "Sir," she said, "we need to speak to you about the noise. Can you open up so we can talk?"

O'Keefe picked up the remote, muted the TV, and opened the door, giving his best smile.

The woman, who looked Eastern European, smiled back. "Sir, I'm sorry, but we've had a complaint about the noise. We don't allow too much noise as we have seven hundred guests within the hotel on any given night, and it's not fair to the other guests."

O'Keefe forced a fake smile. "You're absolutely right. It isn't fair. Apologies. I just got into town. I think I need to lie down."

O'Keefe shut the door, still smiling. He wanted to rip the door off its hinges and throw it headfirst through his window.

His cell phone rang.

"And so the time has come." The voice of Thomas "Mad Dog" Mills.

"Let's do this."

"Fuck them up good, bro. Blood in, blood out."

The line went dead.

O'Keefe's heart was racing. He went over to the filthy bed, opened the backpack again, and pulled out the rifle, scope, and magazine and ammo. Reassembled it all. The cold steel against his warm skin was reassuring. Then he opened a side zip pocket and pulled out a bottle of Gatorade heavily spiked with methamphetamine.

He rifled through the backpack and pulled out a travel garment bag. They had thought of everything. He laid it on the bed carefully, unzipped it, and pulled out the contents.

O'Keefe smiled as he inspected a dark-navy NYPD uniform, a badge, and shiny black shoes.

Thirty-Three

Lauren Reznick stood at the intersection of Seventh Avenue and West Forty-Fourth Street, being jostled by the huge Times Square crowds. Steam billowed out of subway grates into the air, still hot even after the sun had gone down. Her cell phone vibrated in her pocket.

"Hey, Dad, how are you?"

"I'm fine. More importantly, how are you? Are you still with your friends in Times Square?"

"They went to a café. That's where I'm headed. We're going to have something to eat and then catch the subway home."

"Where are you?"

Lauren gave her location. "That's where the café is. Satisfied?"

"First, get yourself into the café. Inside, away from the window. At the very least."

"I got it."

"There was another shooting close to Penn Station."

"I saw that on Twitter."

"The perp is still on the loose. And he's in or around Times Square. You need to get inside or back to your apartment. Do not be out in the open, exposed."

"I'm literally walking to the Europa Café. I'm about one hundred yards from it."

J. B. Turner

"I'm going to stay on the line until you confirm to me that you are out of sight. And well away from the window."

"Got it."

Lauren passed a hotel and saw the lights of the café. She headed inside.

"Are you finally inside?"

"Yes, I'm inside. I'm shutting the door behind me as we speak."

"Are your friends there?"

"Yeah, I can see them now. They're not near the window. And they're drinking coffee and eating muffins and sandwiches."

"Lucky them. Right, stay there for now. And then leave the Times Square area. Walk over to Ninth Avenue, catch a cab, and get back to your apartment."

Lauren's friends waved her over to their table, and she pulled out a seat as a waitress approached. "Hang on, Dad." She ordered a latte and a ham sandwich on rye. "Thank you."

"You're making me hungry," Reznick said.

"What happened today?" Lauren asked.

"I can't tell you right now. But I will . . ."

"When? I want to know."

Her father sighed. "Later. When this is over. There's one guy still on the loose."

"What does he look like?"

A pause. "Aryan Brotherhood. They're very distinctive."

"Seriously?"

"The youngest brother of the two nutcases that killed the cops outside Yankee Stadium. He killed the two cops in the Financial District. And the attorney general."

Lauren went quiet.

"Now do you see why I want you to get the hell out of there?"

"I understand that, Dad."

208

"This guy on the loose is hyper-violent. He has nothing to lose. Nothing."

"Dad, I'm out of sight."

"So, stay where you are."

"Will do. We're fine. There are cops on every corner. Where are you?"

"Not far. Couple hundred yards. Maybe less."

"You want to join us for coffee and sandwiches?"

"Maybe another time."

Two shots rang out on the street. Then the screaming began.

"What was that, Lauren?"

Lauren saw people running down the street. "Shots fired! Did you hear that, Dad?"

"Get down! Hide! Do not make a move! I'm on my way!"

Thirty-Four

Reznick could still hear the sound of semiautomatic gunfire coming through his cell phone. He was running down Seventh Avenue. Dodging cars and cabs as he sprinted across Broadway at Forty-Fifth Street. "Stay on the line, Lauren!"

"I will, Dad."

"Do not make a run for it!" Reznick said. "Is there a basement or storeroom to hide out in?"

He was close enough to the Europa Café to hear more rifle shots. Then high-pitched screaming.

"Man down, Dad!" Lauren said. Her voice was surprisingly calm, authoritative. "One cop down. Outside Hard Rock Cafe. Two cops. I repeat, two cops! More, maybe, I think."

"Stay right where you are. Do you understand? Do not move! Keep down! Out of sight! Away from windows!"

"People out on the street are pointing up at a building farther down West Forty-Third. I think he's really close to us."

"He's probably firing from a high floor close to you. Now listen . . ."

More shots. People were running in every direction.

"Dad, he's hit another cop, he's bleeding out. He's been shot, crawling outside."

"Leave him be! Stay inside! Do you hear? Do not attend to him. Under no circumstances are you to make a move at this time!"

"He's losing blood."

Fleeing pedestrians were slamming into Reznick. It was like trying to run against the ocean's current. "Lauren, listen to me!"

"I can see him. I need to get him off the street."

Reznick felt rising panic as he raced toward the location. "Lauren! Do not break cover! Stay put! Help is on the way! I'm nearly there."

Suddenly, the line went dead. He put his phone back in his pocket. He was going out of his mind.

His earpiece crackled to life. "Jon, it's Martha. Gunshots on West Forty-Third Street! Repeat, gunshots on Forty-Third Street. Officers down. Repeat. Five officers down."

Reznick barged past a swarm of people. "Copy that. I'm a block away. Lauren is in a café nearby. I just spoke to her."

"What? Are you sure?"

"Affirmative. She's there right now. I'm closing in."

"The ESU is headed there, on foot."

But for Reznick, as he ran those last hundred yards, struggling to get past the huge panicking crowds, his mind was in a free fall with worry for his daughter.

Thirty-Five

Lauren's friends grabbed her arm as she tried to leave the café. Customers huddled under tables and behind the counter.

"Don't be so stupid, Lauren! Stay here, that's what your dad said!"

Lauren pulled her arm away. She would not cower in fear. Her father had instilled that in her.

"Are you insane? Get down!"

"What the hell is wrong with you all?"

A man hiding behind a table pointed at her. "Do not fucking go out there, lady, do you hear me? You'll put us all at risk."

"There's an injured man out there. What's wrong with you?"

Lauren looked out the café window at the people fleeing the scene. She could see five injured officers, one only yards from the café, blood pouring from his mouth. He was reaching out as if trying to crawl to safety. Sirens blared.

A woman behind the counter reached over and gave Lauren a pile of hand towels.

Lauren pushed open the door and ran to the officer. He looked up, eyes glassy. She could hear screaming coming from everywhere. She pressed the towels tight against his neck wound and turned around. "Please, someone," she said. "He's lost a lot of blood! Someone call 911!"

It was a surreal scene in which everything seemed slowed down. Dead and dying victims. Lights. Chaos.

People ignored the dying officer as they ran past. She turned and looked down the street and saw people peering down from the windows and roofs of adjacent buildings, filming on their cell phones. "Why won't anyone help this officer? We need to get him to a hospital."

A police officer carrying a bottle of Gatorade kneeled down beside her. "Quick! Take his legs and I'll take his arms. Get him in my car over there!"

"Thank you, Officer. Are you hurt?"

"I'm fine. Just got here."

Lauren and the man lifted the bleeding cop into the back of a police car.

"Get in the back with him," he said. "Let's get him to a hospital."

Lauren did as she was told.

The cop started up the car and sped off down West Forty-Third Street, blue lights on, running the lights until Ninth Avenue. Then he took a left, nearly knocking down a couple in the crosswalk.

Lauren glanced at the rearview mirror and noticed the guy's eyes were bloodshot and glazed. "Where are we going? There's no hospital over here."

The cop turned around and pointed a gun at her head. "Stop whining and shut the fuck up."

Thirty-Six

Reznick saw the bloodied bodies of cops strewn across West Forty-Third Street, bathed in the red and blue lights of ambulances and cop cars. Paramedics and other cops and passersby worked frantically to treat the officers. He shoved through the crowds on the sidewalk, past a hotel, and finally got to the café.

He went inside and people were screaming, near hysterical.

"FBI!" he shouted. "Do not move until this area is secured. Is that understood? You need to pay attention and not move from here."

There was sobbing from some of the customers.

"We'll get you out of here when we can. But I'm also looking for Lauren Reznick. I'm her father." He looked around, people hugging each other, petrified. "Anyone?"

A twentysomething black girl pointed outside. "She went to help an officer. We told her not to."

Reznick's heart sank. "So where is she?"

A Hispanic man behind the counter said, "I saw her getting in the back of a cop car with the injured cop."

"And a cop was driving the car?"

"Yes, he was. Positive."

Reznick felt a wave of relief that she was alive. He went out on the street and saw the ESU team pouring into a hotel. He saw Fogerty, the young guy he met earlier. "Hey, Danny, what's going on?"

"Shooter on a high floor."

"Is he still there?"

"We don't know. I heard a report a few moments ago that he might have fled. But he might also be hiding out. We're gonna check it out."

Reznick patted him on the back. "Best of luck, son."

The ESU guy stormed past him and into the hotel as Reznick surveyed the scene on West Forty-Third Street. It was like a war zone. His mind flashed back to Fallujah, all those years ago. Bodies strewn on the backstreets. Fallen soldiers. Dead civilians. Screaming. Dying. Blood.

His earpiece crackled to life.

"Jon, it's Martha!"

"Shooter might be gone, according to one of the ESU guys. And we've got bodies everywhere on West Forty-Third. It's like a scene from hell."

"It's even worse than that."

"What do you mean?"

"We're piecing together a sequence of events from surveillance cameras. O'Keefe is wearing a cop uniform."

The words skidded across his mind in slow motion. "No!"

"I'm looking at the still image now. Two minutes forty-three seconds ago. Lauren is helping him lift an injured cop into the back of a police cruiser."

Panic and a sense of dread began to set in. "Jesus, no!"

"The uniform helped O'Keefe blend in as he left. Made it look plausible, especially by having him and a bystander, Lauren, carry a dying cop away from the scene."

"Where is the vehicle? I need to know! Which way did they go? Tell me!"

"We have it headed south on Ninth Avenue." She hesitated. "Into the Lincoln Tunnel."

Reznick turned and began sprinting toward Ninth Avenue. "Martha, stay on the line. You need to stay on the line."

"Jon, we've alerted New Jersey cops. They're handling it."

"I don't give a shit. That's my daughter."

Reznick was running down the Midtown street, ignoring the snarled-up traffic, crowds, and chaos. He felt his heart racing like it was going to explode. But he ran even faster. He had to get to Lauren.

A sense of foreboding washed over him, filling him with a terrible, sickening dread.

Thirty-Seven

Lauren was desperately trying to stem the bleeding of the NYPD officer lying sprawled on the back seat of the speeding car. She pressed the towels against his throat. He was gargling blood, trying to speak. She turned and looked at the man reflected in the rearview mirror.

The driver, dressed as a cop, gulped down the Gatorade and grinned. Eyes crazy wide, pupils dilated. His lower arm was exposed, showing an Aryan Brotherhood tattoo. "Well, this is fun, huh? Helluva day in New York City, right?"

Lauren felt panicky. She wondered how she had been so stupid. "Please, you need to get this police officer to a hospital."

"And that's exactly where I'm taking him."

"Are you serious?"

The driver laughed as if he had lost his mind. "No. Absolutely not. I'm going to let that fucker bleed out in his own patrol car. What do you think of that?"

"This man is no threat to you. He needs immediate treatment."

"He's going to die like a dog. That's what he is. The motherfucker!"

Lauren looked at the injured officer. His eyes were rolling around in his head as if he were struggling to stay conscious. The driver sped on, headed through the Lincoln Tunnel and into Union City, New Jersey, negotiating the sharp turns. "Who are you?" she asked.

"Listen, honey, I'm not going to kill a nice white girl like you. But you need to understand that the cops, like the one bleeding out, killed my father in cold blood. My father! How would you like that to happen to your father?"

The dying cop's eyes were filled with tears.

Lauren pressed the blood-soaked towels tighter. She whispered, "Please hang in there, Officer. Stay with us. Do you understand?"

The driver began to laugh and mimicked her voice. "*Stay with us!* Gimme a break, will you? Listen to yourself. You think he cares about you? He cares about his salary. About his standing in the community. His pension. His bowling on a Tuesday night. His fucking St. Paddy's Day Parade pipes and drums bullshit."

"For God's sake," Lauren snapped, "what is wrong with you?"

The driver reached around and pointed the gun at her forehead again, one hand on the wheel, eyes on the road. "You wanna know? You really want to know?"

Lauren wondered if she might be able to shove the gun aside and escape. But she knew she could be seriously injured or killed if she tried it. Besides, the officer would die too. She needed to keep the shooter talking. "Yes, I do want to know. Tell me."

"The cops ripped the heart out of my family. Don't you fucking understand? Can you comprehend what I'm saying?"

Lauren nodded.

The driver glanced in the rearview mirror. "I can look at your face and see you don't get it. I can look into your eyes and see everything there is to know about you. I bet you were brought up with lots of money. And you sure as hell don't care for me, my kind, or my father. What do you know about loss? What do you know about anything?"

"I lost my mother on 9/11. Happy?"

"Well, I apologize, maybe you do understand my anger. My hurt. Maybe I've misread you."

"Please, you need to stop. What you're doing is wrong. It's disgusting."

"Oh, listen to little Miss Butter Wouldn't Melt in My Fucking Mouth! You think you've got a right to judge me? To sit in judgment of me or my family? Until you've walked in my shoes, you don't know shit."

Lauren focused on the cop, trying to ignore the madman. Warm blood had seeped through the towels onto her hands. Her mind flashed to the images of the falling towers on 9/11. A cataclysmic mass terrorist attack. She began to think of her mother again. Her final helpless moments. Had she been trapped high up in the tower in lower Manhattan? Had she said a silent prayer? Had she thought of her baby daughter at that moment? What was she thinking in those desperate last minutes? And now, all these years later, Lauren herself was staring into the abyss on the streets of New York. On the Fourth of July of all days.

She had to think. She needed a plan. And she needed to stay alive. She wasn't going to go down without a fight. Her mother had never had a chance. But she did.

"They'll be looking for me. Hunting me down. But I'm ready for them. I think I might've bought some time. Maybe be able to disappear up north. Canada."

"They'll catch you. You'd be better off surrendering."

The driver began to laugh. "The moment you stop fighting is the moment you surrender. I don't surrender. To you or anyone. I fight. I survive."

His insane eyes found hers in the rearview mirror. "Bet you don't bump into too many Aryan Brotherhood guys where you come from. Bet we're not the kind of guys you usually hang out with, am I right?"

"Please," she said, "I'm begging you, just drop us off, I'll get him out, and you can drive off."

"Just like that, huh?"

"I'm asking you for mercy."

"Mercy? Like the mercy the cops showed when they strangled my father? He was screaming for air, but *they* didn't give a damn about mercy."

"Please, you need to let us out."

"I don't need to do anything. Your voice reminds me of a teacher I used to have. She never liked me because I never listened to her. Blabbing away. Why don't you just shut the fuck up? This is probably the most fun you've had in your whole fucking wretched life!"

The driver began to laugh some more. "Helluva day in New York City."

Thirty-Eight

Reznick was sitting in the back of an SUV, squashed in with a couple of Feds as they sped across the west side of Manhattan and down into the Lincoln Tunnel. The lights of the tunnel and beams from oncoming vehicles flashed by. His mind was racing like an out-of-control freight train. He thought of Lauren at the mercy of that sick maniac. He wondered how she was coping. He imagined she would be trying to reason with him. She would need to think critically. But as Reznick knew only too well, even the best-laid plans could turn to dust in the blink of an eye.

He ran scenarios around and around in his head. She would be fighting to remain calm and trying not to freak out or do something rash. Hopefully she was keeping O'Keefe talking. What worried Reznick most was the state of mind of the killer holding her hostage. He would be crazed like a rabid dog. Maybe drugged up. Out of his fucking mind. Maybe high on ice. Meth. Which would make him far, far more dangerous and unpredictable.

Dark thoughts flashed through Reznick's mind. His deepest, blackest fears. The fear that he would lose Lauren. That dread was never far from the surface. It led him to a place he would rather not think of.

The Fed beside him said, "We'll find her, I promise."

Reznick nodded as his mood oscillated between his natural fears as a father and the logical, clinical, compartmentalized focus of an assassin.

He wondered if Lauren would try to jump out of the car. He hoped and prayed she wouldn't be that desperate. But who could blame her? The reality was that she would end up, best-case scenario, seriously injured, maybe paralyzed. No, it was better for her to remain a hostage until he got there.

Reznick looked at the car's dashboard. They were doing a leisurely sixty miles per hour. He was dying to take the wheel. Take over. He was a control freak. He knew that. And he wasn't coping well knowing events were out of his control. He felt as if he were going out of his fucking mind. Nightmares stirred within the darkest recesses of his thoughts.

He shifted in his seat, frustrated that they were trailing in the guy's wake. The lack of urgency was killing him. But so was the fact that they still had no precise fix on the guy's position, only knew that he had made it through the Lincoln Tunnel.

Reznick was nearly certain that O'Keefe was using a sophisticated military jammer in some sort of capacity, knocking out wireless surveillance cameras, GPS, and anything in its path.

"Do you want to step on it?" he said to the driver.

"We're doing nearly seventy."

"Jesus Christ, move it! What's wrong with you? It feels like we're going backward. Get a fucking move on!"

"Jon, relax," the driver said. "We'll get him."

"Don't tell me to relax when my daughter is at risk. You do understand that she's in the back of the fucking cop car with that maniac? Floor it!"

The driver finally began to accelerate through the tunnel. "We're close, Jon."

"Not close enough."

The Fed sitting beside Reznick in the back seat was now on his cell phone, deep in conversation. "Yeah, he's here." He handed the phone to Reznick. "It's for you."

"Who is it?"

"The Director."

"O'Donoghue?"

The Fed nodded, grim faced. "Yeah."

Reznick took the cell phone. "Sir, what's the latest?"

"Jon, I'm terribly sorry about what's happening. But I wanted you to know that we are doing everything in our power to locate O'Keefe's vehicle."

"New Jersey cops on it?"

"Everyone is on this. And I mean everyone. We will find him. And your daughter. Every resource at our disposal, other agencies—we're calling on all of it."

Reznick closed his eyes, struggling to contain the rage building up inside him.

"It's been a terribly dark day for New York, Jon. For America. But you've done a helluva job."

"That will all count for nothing if I don't find my daughter alive and stop that animal."

"I'm a father too, I get it. We will find him. And your daughter."

"Thank you, sir."

"Martha is listening in on this call. She wants to speak to you."

Reznick felt his throat tighten. He sensed events were moving fast and out of his control.

"We've blocked all traffic headed out of Union City except for the FBI," Meyerstein said when she came on the line. "Their current location is headed south on Palisades Avenue. Perhaps heading for Hoboken."

"Copy that," said Reznick.

"Jon, this is bad luck. Bad, bad luck. But I know you'll get him."

Reznick stared out of the car window as they raced through the dark streets of Union City. No one knew how it was going to end. He wanted to confide in Meyerstein about how he felt. He wanted to talk to her about so many things. He wanted to tell her how terrified he was of losing his girl. He knew in his heart that if Lauren died, he would surely die too.

He wanted to tell her that. To tell her how he felt. He wanted to open up to her. He knew he was a closed book. He wasn't the type of guy who shared his feelings. But he wanted to tell her about his guilt for buying Lauren tickets for the Yankees game. It was dumb to even think like that. But that's how he felt, consumed by blind terror and fear of the unknown.

"Jon?"

Reznick stared out at a desolate street in Union City. "Yeah, I'm still here."

"I just wanted to say we're here, and we will find her."

Thirty-Nine

The cop was bleeding out in the back seat of the stolen NYPD cruiser, and there was nothing Lauren could do about it. She cradled his neck as she continued to try to stem the blood loss. The car jolted every time they sped over a manhole cover or a pothole. The officer moaned loudly.

She couldn't abandon the dying cop. She just couldn't. She hoped and prayed they would crash and be knocked unconscious, and the sick bastard driver would have to make a run for it. But darker thoughts were also crowding her shattered mind.

Lauren had begun to contemplate her own death. The officer had lost a lot of blood and was slipping away.

Her thoughts began to drift. She began to wonder if her friends in the café were safe. Had they seen her take the injured cop into the car? She thought of her father. He'd been only blocks away when it happened. She could imagine his reaction. He would be horrified. And furious at her for not listening to him.

He was the one who'd warned her not to go outside, fearing she'd be hit by a sniper's bullet. As it turned out, she'd been tricked by the sniper. But she still lived in the hope that her father would find her. Somehow. Some way.

The seconds felt like hours.

Must do something.

Lauren closed her eyes as she struggled to cope with the perilous nature of her situation. She needed to focus. She needed to get a grip. She couldn't expect help to arrive. And even if it did, it might be too late. She needed to act.

The driver glanced in the rearview mirror. "New Jersey, huh? Gotta love it."

"Let us out, for God's sake! He's going to die!"

"Good. Then his wife and kids will know what loss and grief feels like."

Lauren looked down at the officer. His mouth was slightly open, blood trickling down his chin. Slowly, his eyes moved to the side. She followed his gaze. His bloody right index finger was pointing to his equipment belt. She looked at the handcuffs, radio, flashlight, chemical spray, and gun holster.

The cop was pointing to the gun on his belt. Had to be that.

She said, "I need to get him more comfortable or he's going to bleed out right now. I need to adjust his position."

The driver took a hard left, screeching around a corner. There was a sudden clanking sound, like hail. He struggled to get the steering under control. "Fuckers! Taken out a rear tire! Fuckers!"

Lauren realized a shot had been fired at their car. She felt a surge of hope. She pressed the blood-soaked towels tight against the officer's neck. He winced and groaned at the pain. Then slowly, she began to reach toward his equipment belt.

Forty

The SUV was hurtling through the dark streets of Union City. Reznick sat in silence. He couldn't bear to think that they would be too late to save his daughter. Lights flashed as a cop car sped past them. They hit ninety as they negotiated a narrow street, headed toward Hoboken.

The Fed beside him was again deep in conversation on his cell phone. "Got it." He turned to Reznick. "They've got a visual. They put a bullet into the rear tire. He might manage a mile or two. So it's just a matter of time."

Reznick felt numb. His daughter, his only child, was still in the car with that psychopath and a dying cop. It couldn't end this way for her. Not now. It wasn't her time. He envisioned the scene unfolding. He imagined he would get one clear shot if they got within sight of O'Keefe. But he was also beginning to consider the horrific possibility that Lauren could be killed. Either by the crazed gunman or by a cop.

The Fed was speaking again into the cell phone. "Ma'am, here he is." He handed Reznick the phone. "Assistant director wants you."

"Martha, what's the latest?"

"The car is slowing down. New Jersey cops have him in their sights. You're not far away. But this is, as you can imagine, a very precarious situation."

Reznick said, "I know. The cops need to ease up, not get too close, or he's going to take a potshot at one of them, or worse, at my daughter, if he hasn't already."

The Fed said to the driver, "One mile and closing. Hudson Street, Hoboken."

Meyerstein said, "Jon, I think this might be out of your hands now."

Reznick sensed his daughter's life was hanging in the balance, only God watching over her. He closed his eyes for a moment and said a silent prayer. "I know. That's what worries me."

Forty-One

The crazy driver who had stolen the cop car was now laughing like a maniac, gritting his teeth. He was drugged. Manic. He had gone Jekyll and Hyde on her. Not good.

"You kids alright back there?" he taunted. "Gone all quiet on me."

Lauren's hand reached toward the dying cop's leather holster. A hard slap rocked her face.

The driver had leaned over and hit her on the cheek. He had seen what she was doing. He reached back in anger now, one hand on the wheel, took the cop's gun from the holster, and threw it on the floor of the front passenger seat. "That what you were looking for?"

Lauren looked down into the cop's eyes. The officer was trying to open his bloody lips, trying to say something.

The driver snapped, "Think I'm fucking stupid, bitch?" He wound down the window and fired at a cop car that was coming up on them in the adjacent lane. "Think old Todd is some dumb peckerwood? Is that it? Just a dumb fucking white shitkicker, is that it?"

Lauren knew she had lost her only chance.

"I'm going to have two dead fucks in the back of a cop car!" He was laughing, crazed, deranged. Shaking his head. Screaming like a banshee. Howling like a wolf. He was out of his mind. "Redneck cocaine, they call it. I love it. Should try it someday, honey. Mix it with an energy drink. What a fucking ride!"

Lauren wiped blood from the officer's lips with the back of her hand. "I'm so sorry."

The driver said, "Give me some ice! I love me some ice! We all wanna go and do some ice!"

Lauren closed her eyes for a moment, trying to block out the crazy bastard driving them to their deaths.

The dying cop's breathing was getting more labored as the police sirens and flashing lights closed in.

Lauren stroked the officer's hair. She wondered if the pursuing cops were just tailing the car until the psycho ran out of gas. She wished they would just try and take him out. But she understood their reluctance to get too close, with a seriously injured cop and Lauren as hostages in the back seat.

The driver glanced in the rearview mirror. "What are you thinking now? Are you going to attack me with handcuffs? Maybe the spray? Well, don't fucking think about it, bitch, or you'll get blown away. I mean, this isn't your fight, is it? What the hell were you thinking? A dying cop? What's he to you?"

Lauren looked down at the cop. His eyes were closed. Tears ran down her cheeks. She pressed the towels against the terrible neck wound, praying for the nightmare to be over.

The officer's hooded eyes opened, tears spilling onto his face.

"I'm sorry," she said again.

The officer's eyes flitted from side to side. Then fixed on his feet.

Lauren thought he was trying to tell her something.

A shot rang out, and the car jolted as if another tire had been shot. They heard the screech of metal dragging. The fender sounded like it was hanging off.

Lauren reached toward the officer's lower leg. That was when she realized there was another gun holster around his right ankle. Her hands were hidden from the driver's sight.

"Fuck is going on back there, bitch?"

"I'm scared I'm going to die!" she said.

The driver began to laugh. "Oh . . . boo-hoo, I'm going to fucking have to die! Well, you know what, we've all got to die. Me, you, and that cop. We all die. Deal with it."

Lauren began to sob as more and more police sirens pierced the air. She looked up through the back window, tears blurring the city streets. A sharp left turn threw Lauren onto her side.

She had her chance.

She pulled up the officer's trouser leg, unbuttoned the small holster, and took out the compact Glock 26. She knew how to use weapons. She'd trained at gun ranges. She racked the slide. Then flicked off the safety.

Lauren turned and pointed the gun at the driver's head.

The driver turned around.

Lauren fired three shots, point-blank, in a deafening series of explosions. Blood sprayed across the shattered windshield. The driver slumped over the steering wheel as the car horn blared. Suddenly, the car veered wildly out of control and smashed headlong into the side of a parked truck.

Lauren was flung around like a rag doll. The driver's airbag inflated. Alarms went off around the street.

Lauren could barely hear. Everything was muffled. Time seemed to stop. She smelled metallic sulfur. The car doors opened. Flashlights and guns appeared, trained on her.

She felt herself being dragged from the vehicle. Blue lights, red lights, streetlights spiraling as she lay motionless on the streets of Hoboken, staring up at the stars in the sky.

Forty-Two

The seconds that followed were an insane blur of lights, faces. Then came an eruption of sounds. Lauren could hear sirens and shouting and someone screaming for backup. Her brain was sending a signal to her body to move. But she lay paralyzed on the sidewalk. She tried to rationalize her reaction. Was she going into deep shock? A paramedic was shouting for the cops to give them more room.

A fresh-faced cop with a flashlight stood over her. "Can you hear what I'm saying, Miss Reznick?"

Lauren just stared up at him. She tried to speak. But nothing emerged.

"Don't worry," he said, "the driver is dead."

Out of the corner of her eye, she saw the bleeding cop she had tended being lifted onto a gurney and into the back of an ambulance.

Lauren felt herself beginning to shake. Flashbacks to the three shots she had fired exploded through her mind. The blood splatter. Time began to almost rewind. Images of the driver's head being torn apart, fragments, brain matter. Like high-definition slow motion.

She sensed someone else was watching her. Someone was holding her hand.

"Lauren!" A familiar voice.

She somehow managed to turn her head. Looking down on her, smiling, was her father. He kneeled down, head bowed. "Thank God, Lauren." He stroked her hair. Like he had when she was a little girl.

Lauren felt his hand on her forehead. His eyes were the bluest she had ever seen. "I got him, Dad," she whispered. "I got him. I got him."

Her dad cradled her head and pulled her close, tears spilling down his face. "I knew you would, Lauren. I knew you would."

Lauren felt herself being lifted up and onto a gurney. She turned and her father's face was touching hers. "Is it over, Dad?"

"It's all over. You're safe now."

Epilogue

Three months later, Jon Reznick was sitting beside his daughter, patiently waiting in a private room on the fourteenth floor of 1 Police Plaza in lower Manhattan, headquarters of the NYPD. The autumn sky outside was a pale blue. He wore a navy suit, white shirt, black Oxford shoes polished to a deep shine, black tie. He looked at his daughter, demure, wearing a navy dress and her late mother's pearl earrings. She had been in therapy since her ordeal at O'Keefe's hands. But she was slowly getting back to the confident young woman she'd been before the terrible series of events on July 4.

The days following her kidnapping had been particularly tough for Lauren—more so, he thought, than after she'd been in a coma and nearly died. She'd headed back to Rockland and begun her recuperation. She walked and walked with Reznick, the sea a constant companion. The familiar salty air refreshing and energizing her. It was far from the hectic streets of New York City. But every night it was the same: Lauren awoke in a cold sweat, screaming, suffering flashbacks and nightmares.

Reznick knew a former army psychologist who specialized in PTSD, and put Lauren in touch with him. The psychologist began to talk with her. She opened up. She talked about the incident. He listened, and gradually, she developed coping mechanisms to deal with the flashbacks.

Lauren began to meditate and did yoga. Slowly she began to heal. It was a long-term project. But at least she was alive, and she was moving in the right direction. She seemed calmer and was even starting to want to talk to Reznick about her ordeal.

The psychologist recommended she attend therapy in Vermont after returning to college in the fall.

Reznick leaned over and held her hand. "Your mother would have been very proud of what you did."

Lauren sighed. "I hope so."

"I know so."

Lauren cleared her throat and gazed at the floor, lost in her thoughts of that long summer day.

"I always meant to ask," he said, "and don't answer if you don't want to . . ."

"What?"

"Maybe I shouldn't ask, I'm sorry. I know you've moved on."

"No, ask me, Dad. My therapist says it's an important part of my rehabilitation to talk openly about it all."

"How did you feel in those minutes, trapped in that car with that crazy bastard, knowing he could kill you whenever he wanted?"

"How did I feel? I felt alone. No one there to help me. And I was scared." She looked at him and smiled. "Dad, you couldn't have done any more on that day."

"I could've been with you. I should've stayed with you instead of going after the first two snipers. And this wouldn't have happened."

"Other people needed you. Besides, it happened for a reason, I think. It's made me look at my life differently. What I want from it."

Reznick smiled back at her.

"You know when I was in the car with him? I thought about what you always said. About working the problem. Trying to figure it out."

"Did you consider all your options?"

"I guess."

"Bet that included considering whether you should jump out of the car or not."

Lauren nodded. "Yes, it did. But I figured I would end up dead or seriously messed up."

Reznick nodded and smiled. "You're absolutely right."

"I tried to weigh it out. But there were no good choices."

"Smart girl. What you did was some serious critical thinking."

Lauren blushed the way her mother had when embarrassed. "I don't know about that."

"You figured you would have a better chance of staying alive by staying put in the car. Waiting for the right moment."

"Correct."

"But you also got the gun. The spare gun. That was smart. Killer smart."

"I got lucky."

"What do I always say, Lauren? Sometimes, you make your own luck. You were looking for something to take the guy down with. And you found it."

"What would you have done differently, Dad?"

Reznick sighed. "Hard to say. I probably would have found a way to grab the gun he was holding, twist it out of his hands, and disarm him. But that's easier said than done. O'Keefe was strong, drugged up, right?"

"Yes, he was. I didn't stand a chance."

Reznick felt his throat tighten as he thought again of Lauren at the mercy of that maniac. "You nailed him. Good and proper."

"Would Mom have done the same in those circumstances?"

Reznick smiled. "Your mother, God rest her soul, would have done exactly what you did. Except for one small point, I think."

"And what's that?"

"She would've emptied the whole magazine clip into him."

Lauren burst out laughing.

"I'm not joking. She was a very determined, smart, and tough woman. And you're just like her."

"There is one way I'm not like her."

"And what's that?"

"I don't want to be a lawyer."

"Fair enough. So, you had the internship experience in publishing. Is that where you're headed?"

Lauren shook her head. "No."

"Really? Thought that was where your future lay."

"It was. Things changed."

"What?"

"I've been seeking out some professional career advice."

Reznick nodded, impressed.

"And I've also asked her if I can let you know . . ."

"Her? Let me know what?"

"Let you know that I've been taking advice from Assistant Director Meyerstein."

Reznick looked at his daughter, struggling to take it in. "Since when?"

"Just the last few weeks. She had my number. I had hers. And I reached out to her."

"You did?"

Lauren nodded. "She's smart. She went to Duke. And I was thinking, maybe the FBI would suit me better."

"You're thinking of joining the FBI?"

"Yeah, I am. Do you have a problem with that?"

Reznick took a few moments for the news to sink in. He shrugged. "If that's what you want, Lauren, I fully support you. The only advice I would give you is to do what you want. If that's the route you want to take, then that's the route you've got to take. Do it."

"I've already inquired about the Collegiate Hiring Initiative for when I'm finished at Bennington."

Reznick smiled and hugged her tight. "You're sure not wasting any time."

"I'm hoping the assistant director is going to be my mentor."

"Your mentor? I guess you've got it all figured out."

Lauren blushed again. "We'll see."

A few moments later, Meyerstein herself entered the room. She wore a navy suit, a pale-pink blouse, and pointed navy shoes. She smiled at them both. "I think they're waiting for the Reznicks."

Reznick turned to look at Lauren. "You ready?"

"I got this, Dad."

"Then let's do it."

They followed Meyerstein out of the small waiting room, down a long corridor, and into the huge fourteenth-floor office of NYPD police commissioner Jimmy Mulroy.

Standing beside Commissioner Mulroy were the governor of New York and the mayor of New York City. Each took their turn to shake Reznick's and his daughter's hands and give a word of thanks and appreciation.

The governor then took a few minutes to recall the "terrible" events that had unfolded in July.

Reznick and Lauren stood in front of them, listening intently. They were both presented with New York's highest civilian award for exceptional citizenship and outstanding achievement, the Bronze Medallion.

The governor pinned the medal on Reznick. "I feel very humbled, Mr. Reznick. What you did, single-handed, that day was above and beyond any bravery I've read about."

"I did what I could, sir, that's all."

"Thank God you did."

The commissioner stepped forward and spoke in reverential tones to Reznick, thanking him profusely. The mayor took a few minutes to chat with him as if they were old friends.

Reznick soaked up the bullshit, feeling distinctly uncomfortable at all the praise. It wasn't his style.

When he had gotten the invitation, his first instinct had been to turn it down. He wasn't a fan of ceremonies and formalities. He was an under-the-radar kind of guy who liked to sidestep that kind of thing. But on reflection, he knew that it was both disrespectful to the people of New York, in whose name the medal was given, and to the families of the fallen officers, if he didn't turn up. But what he did ask was for the ceremony to be strictly private—no media, no photographs, no PR. And his request had been granted.

The governor pinned the medal on Lauren and shook her hand. "Young lady, it takes some guts to do what you did. We're all so proud of you. But perhaps more than anything, your heroic attempts to save Officer Bryce on West Forty-Third Street, when everyone else was running for cover amid the shootings and carnage, were exemplary."

Lauren gave a polite nod. "Thank you, sir."

The commissioner stepped forward and shook her hand. "Great job, Miss Reznick."

Lauren again gave a polite nod. "Thank you, sir."

Finally, the mayor said, "There is someone else who wants to say thank you. I hope you don't mind."

The office door opened.

NYPD officer Fergus Bryce entered in a wheelchair, resplendent in a smart navy police uniform, his wife by his side. They were flanked by four beautiful kids.

Bryce looked up at Lauren and shook her hand. "You saved my life, Miss Reznick. I owe you so much. I owe you everything. So does my family. We're truly blessed."

Lauren blinked away the tears as his wife stepped forward and hugged her tight before the children did too.

Reznick stood and watched, heart swelling with pride. The commissioner bowed his head and said a prayer.

When the prayer was finished, Reznick turned around. Standing at the far side of the office was Martha Meyerstein, head held high, smiling back at him.

Reznick walked over to her. "Helluva day."

"Indeed. I'm very glad you decided to come, Jon. I had this idea that you would scrunch up the invite and throw it into Penobscot Bay, just like you did when you got the invite to the White House."

"This is different."

"You could have opted out. I would've understood."

"What? And miss meeting the governor, the commissioner, and the mayor at the same time? Are you kidding me?"

Meyerstein shook her head and rolled her eyes. "I'm glad you got this recognition."

"I'm glad my daughter's alive. And I'm glad you're helping her. She told me all about it. That makes me happy."

Meyerstein sighed and gave a nervous smile. "She's very bright."

"Good shot too."

"Yes, and a helluva good shot too. Jon, I've got some news for you."

Reznick shrugged. "What kind of news?"

"About the report from our SWAT team leader in New York."

"It had crossed my mind."

"You can rest easy. The report didn't mention what you did in Gowanus. Not a word."

Reznick nodded, relieved after having the threat of an FBI investigation hanging over him. "How long have you known?"

"A little while. Wanted to tell you face-to-face. The guy did you a serious favor. You might want to buy him a drink if you ever see him again."

"Did you have anything to do with his decision?"

"I couldn't possibly comment."

"I crossed the line. I know that."

"What's done is done."

Reznick cleared his throat. "I was wondering . . ."

"Wondering . . . wondering about what?"

"Wondering whether you want to go for a drink? That is, if you don't have to fly back down to DC."

"You got anywhere in mind?"

"Lauren mentioned a rooftop bar in the East Village. I was going to take her there for a treat."

"A rooftop bar? You don't strike me as a rooftop bar kind of guy."

"I'm not. But it's a beautiful autumn day in New York, and the bar's got great views, apparently. What do you say? Would you like to join us?"

Meyerstein looked over at Lauren, then back at Reznick. "Count me in, tough guy."

Acknowledgments

I would like to thank my editor, Jack Butler, and everyone at Amazon Publishing for their enthusiasm, hard work, and belief in the Jon Reznick thriller series. I would also like to thank my loyal readers. Thanks also to Faith Black Ross for her terrific work on this book and to Caitlin Alexander in New York, who looked over an early draft.

Last but by no means least, thank you to my family and friends for their encouragement and support. None more so than my wife, Susan.

About the Author

J. B. Turner is a former journalist and the author of the Jon Reznick series of action thrillers (*Hard Road*, *Hard Kill*, *Hard Wired*, *Hard Way*, *Hard Fall*, and *Hard Hit*), the American Ghost series of black-ops thrillers (*Rogue*, *Reckoning*, and *Requiem*), and the Deborah Jones political thrillers (*Miami Requiem* and *Dark Waters*). He has a keen interest in geopolitics. He lives in Scotland with his wife and two children.